Samuel Middleton Fox

Our own Pompeii

Vol. 1

Samuel Middleton Fox

Our own Pompeii
Vol. 1

ISBN/EAN: 9783337347529

Printed in Europe, USA, Canada, Australia, Japan

Cover: Foto ©Andreas Hilbeck / pixelio.de

More available books at **www.hansebooks.com**

OUR OWN POMPEII

A ROMANCE OF TO-MORROW

" Là du plaisant Avril la saisin immortelle
 Sans eschange le suit,
La terre sans labeur, de sa grasse mamelle
 Toute chose y produit,
D'enbas la troupe sainte autrefois amoureuse,
 Nous honorant sur tous,
Viendra nous saluer, s'estimant bien-heureuse
 De s'accointer de nous."
 —PIERRE DE RONSARD.

IN TWO VOLUMES

VOL. I.

WILLIAM BLACKWOOD AND SONS
EDINBURGH AND LONDON
MDCCCLXXXVII

TO

H. M. S. AND R. S.,

IF THEY WILL ACCEPT IT,

THIS LITTLE BOOK IS DEDICATED.

OUR OWN POMPEII.

CHAPTER I.

LONDON Society, about the time that our story opens, was getting a little tired of even its latest amusements. It was hoping, indeed, that some one would be kind enough to invent a new dissipation as soon as possible. It had tried "The Orleans"—had heard of "Almack's"—had danced and been danced to at "The New Club"; and was now primed, as one may say, to go off somewhere else, if only an aim should be given to it.

What could be more lucky, therefore, at this particular moment, than a happy thought that occurred to Mr Smythe, himself one of Society's favoured constituents, whom it condescended to know, on condition that he should devote his talents to its amusements and interests.

For to Mr Smythe (he called himself Smythe, though his real name was Smith) the idea of forming "The Pompeii Club" was due.

It was to be quite unique: a grand international affair, with committees in London, Paris, Vienna, Rome, and New York, to elect its members. It was to be housed in a lovely little city of its very own — built especially for it, in imitation of the classical one, but without a too slavish following of the original. Health, comfort, and exquisite beauty were to mingle in its ideal perfection. Nestling beneath the deep wooded hills—washed by the Mediterranean ripples—it would seem an earthly Paradise of mosaic and marble, of snug chambers and noble halls, of tiny streets and breezy spaces, planned by the best architects, and filled with the brilliant life of choice and charming people.

Mr Smythe, having made up his mind that his Pompeii was feasible, and would be delightful, besides enabling him to show his good nature once more by inventing another distraction for his friends, lost no time in calling upon Lady Marlowe, who, he knew, would enthusiastically take up his plans, and help him to carry them to a successful conclusion.

She was an extremely enterprising member of Society. She boasted that you met a greater number of "nice people" at her parties than at any other house in London. And it was characteristic of her, that although she had many other advantages, this was the only one that she ever mentioned with evident gratification. With a boldness equalled by its success, she had ventured to revive the *salon;* and was "at home" to her friends (among whom it was a privilege to count one's self) every Tuesday during the season.

Discriminating people enjoyed her evenings with a peculiar zest. She gave a certain distinguishing tone or flavour to these by including among her guests a clever, pretty, and intellectual element, "which one never meets anywhere else," everybody said; while at the same time there was always a sufficient contingent of "everybody," to prevent them from feeling that there was "nobody" there.

Both in her friendships and in her life she was
very independent, without being in the least Bohe-
mian. She was well educated and ubiquitously intellectual. She designed art needlework; she sang;
she photographed. In addition to all these acquire-
ments, she had finally shown her taste by acquiring
a certain amount of beauty; and after this proof,
it is needless to add she was very clever. Last,
but not least, she now and then wrote (and got
published) a charming novel, in the most advanced
and approved of our latter-day styles — novels
which busy themselves about four or five highly
developed and brilliantly typical people, with elaborate and much analysed characters, who stay
at or travel to delightful places in Europe, Asia,
and America.

Lady Marlowe was at home; and when Mr
Smythe had described his plans, she felt as though
the crowning moment of her life were come.

"What a lovely place we will have!" she ex-
claimed. "Full of charming people — nothing
but charming people. No tourists, no mob. All
that is most perfect from every country. Why
shouldn't it become a second Athens?"

"We must at any rate be careful that it don't become a second Corinth," said Mr Smythe. "However, I think it a capital plan; and the first thing to be done is to organise the English Committee."

So they set to work with the utmost tact and discretion to sound the "right people" on the subject. Most of the right people thought that it would be delightful if it could be managed— were anxious to be members if the club were really started—though they shrank from being placed on the committee or having their names publicly mixed up with the affair at present.

But Mr Smythe drew such glowing pictures of how delightful, how exclusive, how extremely "smart" it would be; Lady Marlowe discoursed so enthusiastically on the brilliance, the beauty, and the charm of a perfect modern life spent in a lovely and classical city (for she always spoke as though they were going to take up their abode in the ancient city, revived, as if by magic, for their exclusive benefit),—that at last the very "rightest" of the right people were won over, and the preliminary committee was formed.

The Duke of Oxford consented to be on it. Both
Lord Marshford and Lord St Kevan were secured.
Lord Downstreamdown represented the sporting
element; and of course no committee of such a
club would be complete without Jack de Barry,
who, as every one knows, was the smartest man
in London, though nobody quite knows why he
occupied this unique position. For although he
organised dances, played polo at Hurlingham,
yachted at Cowes, shot in Scotland, and, in short,
did the correct thing on the right spot at each
particular moment, all the year round, there were
hundreds of other men doing the same, who were
at the same time showier, cleverer, and more osten-
tatious than he. Some people thought that his
position was due to his having the soles of his
boots blacked (in the French style). Others at-
tributed it to his kind, pleasant, and good-hearted
character — he never said an ill - natured word
about anybody—but they, I fear, were probably
mistaken.

When he joined, success was nearly certain.
And while several other leading people completed
the men's committee, the ladies' division began to

elect the ladies—the election being accompanied by such intrigues, heart-burnings, passionate appeals, and still more passionate imprecations, as the reader may try to imagine, but which cannot be described.

Then diplomatic negotiations were opened up with the various Embassies, committees were arranged in the several capitals of Europe, and the ballot simultaneously set to work over half the world to find out who were the elect and chosen people to form an ideal community, in a city which should bloom forth with every antique perfection and modern luxury.

At length the club was really started. The world in general heard about it with mingled feelings of awe and envy. It was preached against in a fashionable church. The Society papers were divided in their opinions about it—one paper even going so far as to say that it was the last vortex into which a corrupt society, drunk and maddened by luxury and vice, were about to fling themselves, before being hurled to destruction in the whirlpool of retribution. Some offensive nobodies were elected, and a few inoffensive peers were " pilled."

Indeed one duke was so treated, as a capriciously selected token intended to show that the committee were no mere respecters of persons, and selected their members by a nobler and deeper test than that of suitability and position.

It will therefore be at once seen that the whole affair was a tremendous success. There were 5000 members elected, and every member had the right of introducing a friend, if the city were not full already. A perfect site near San Remo had been selected by the provisional committee; and the city was begun at once, from plans prepared by an international committee of architects, who proposed to build it on the plan of Pompeii (the old Pompeii, as it was now called), without slavishly adhering to the original in every detail.

Of course money was a difficulty; but an American gentleman was discovered, of boundless wealth and equally boundless social ambition. It was diplomatically explained to him that, if he would build the city, it might prove a good speculation, in addition to making him a social power and giving him a world-wide reputation as a benefactor of society. However rich a man may be, he can do but

little good in the world in comparison with all the
misery and poverty that weigh down the majority
of the human race. And with such brilliant hopes
of social philanthropy held out to him,.was it likely
that a clever American would forego their realisa-
tion for the sake of a few hundred thousands of
pounds? Having secured the promise of £50,000
in entrance-fees, he at once concluded the bargain.
And the club, being now fixed on every foundation
that could give it stability, began to rise like a
series of fairy palaces among the olive-clad hills
that shelter the Riviera.

By the following spring everything was finished,
and one warm day in February saw the city
really opened. It glittered in the distance like
some poet's vision of dream-wrought loveliness—
its feet lapped by the sunny ripples of its southern
sea, and its walls embraced by deep masses of overhanging foliage, clinging to them and overshadowing them with a flickering canopy of entwining
branches, through which the sunshine broke in little
points of light.

It was approached by a gateway in the wall,
opening directly on to a number of diminutive

streets. They ran in all directions, and were lined by rows of tiny houses, built in exact imitation of the classical ones. Some of them, however, simply consisted of one or more bedrooms, while others had a sitting-room in addition, which could be engaged at the option of the members.

The Stadium was approached from the main street. It was paved, and laid out in lawn-tennis courts, with a track running round for chariot races — an ancient amusement that Mr Smythe hoped to revive. At the sea end of it rose a gymnasium, opening on to a noble swimming-bath. The clear water reflected a stately row of graceful statues, that paused at its brim and bent their beautiful heads over its cool green depths. The whole scene seemed to "compose" with the glowing forms of the happy bathers—swimming, diving, or resting upon the warm pavement—into a living picture of that Hellenic life which has passed away so long.

In the centre of the city was the Forum, paved with mosaic. A charming little stage was built at one end of it, with a proscenium full of tender tints and tones, given by the mingling marbles and the rich drapery of the curtains behind them. The stage was flanked on either side by flights of marble steps leading down to the sea.

And above them might be seen a generous view of grey-green hills and far blue waters, that shone with a dark Southern radiance in the sunshine, and changed, enchanted by the moonlight, into a magic landscape of dreamy light and vague delicious distance.

Along the Forum, on either side of it, were ranged the dining-rooms, coffee-rooms, reading-rooms, and the various other apartments necessary to the collective life of the present day, each built separately in the fashion of an exquisite little classical temple, and painted throughout with frescoes, either copied from those at Pompeii or designed by the best modern artists. In the cool and spacious courts, tiny fountains fell in spray among the gold-fish. Soft fabrics waved in the doorways, or were lifted aside to open out a vision of stately colonnades, corners filled with flowers, and little peeps of blue sky—strangely dark amid the carved cornices, the clustering walls, and the shadowed doorway, that seemed to frame them.

Everything was hushed, and pervaded with the softest, the most luxurious spirit of classical felicity and calm repose. Through the gleaming vestibules and sunlit gardens, graceful and lovely Italian servants, in short clinging classical dresses, passed noiselessly to and fro.

But the splash of fountains, the sound of distant music, and the deep whispers of the distant waves, were not the only sounds that broke the stillness; for a pleasant chatter filled the halls, and indicated that all this was not some memory of buried loveliness, but one that was to yield delight to every one who should come to enjoy it.

Men in all those picturesque costumes of cloth and flannel that comfort can suggest; ladies dressed so perfectly that mute admiration should take the place of description; and ladies dressed (to put it gently) as one might see them anywhere else,— were scattered about among the glancing lights and rich shadows, admiring the buildings, chatting to their friends, or lounging on the comfortable seats and divans that were provided.

Occasionally some one would play a few notes on a piano to try its tone, or knock about the bil-

liard balls in order to see if the tables were level.
There was one old gentleman scanning the wine-list
to assure himself that none of his favourite vintages
were omitted. And several ladies were already inquiring where the fireplace might be looked for in
a classical home, becoming fiercely indignant when
Mr Leo assured them that a bronze pan of charcoal
was more in keeping—helped more to give the true
Roman "note" to the place. One American lady
repeatedly demanded an "elevator"—though where
she wished to be elevated to was not perhaps so
clear. The majority of English ladies declared
that the place was perforated—honeycombed—
with draughts; and one German baron threatened
to resign when he discovered that he could not
close all the windows, because there were no
windows to close.

But in spite of these little *contretemps*, the general murmur of conversation expressed a feeling of
gratified pleasure; and the various little exclam-
ations of delight that fell on the air might be sum-
marised into the constantly recurring phrase of
"How delightful it all is!"

On such a day—warm as a summer's afternoon

in England, yet tempered by the Mediterranean
breeze, with the perfect city at last complete, and
filled with delightful and delighted people—criti-
cism must wholly sink for once into admiration.
And one could not choose a more auspicious
moment than the present for congratulating Lady
Marlowe and Mr Smythe, the various committees,
and the whole of the members, on the brilliant
fulfilment of this happiest of schemes.

CHAPTER II.

THE club was opened in the beginning of March, and the southern French trains were daily filled with members hastening to take up their quarters and assist at its success. On one of these days the corner seat of a first-class carriage was occupied by a young man who divided his attention between a newspaper and the somewhat monotonous view that France provides in such abundance. He was a good-looking young fellow, who combined a great appreciation for all that is "nicest" in life with a careless and winning grace which generally ensured his enjoyment of it, and which endeared him with a peculiar charm to his friends, of whom, it is needless to say, he had a great many. At Harrow he did some work and a great deal of play. And when he went up to Oxford to spend

those happy years which pass like a sunny dream
—filled with so much joy, and friendship, and
beauty, and learning, and buoyant exercise, that
they seem to blend into one sweet memory, one
long spell of poetry and romance — he plunged
into everything with an intellectual excitement
that was stimulated by the harmonious loveliness
around. He worked—as he himself said—when he
had nothing more important to do. He read a
great deal, sitting in the deep window-seat of his
dark-panelled room. He played polo and hunted.
He joined the Bullingdon; spoke sometimes at the
Union; knew many men in many sets; and was
generally called "charming," when an adjective
was required to describe him.

His chief characteristic was an inquiring energy,
a restless activity both of mind and body, that
was almost too unflagging, leading him to inquire
so swiftly into every branch of knowledge he came
across—to find so many "interesting things" to
learn and accomplish — that he had been called
superficial; though it must be added that what
he lost in depth he gained in breadth—in surface,
as it were. He had a character "large enough to

feel the irritation of small precautions"; and it therefore may not seem surprising that his relations, with that perversity which is sometimes found among even the best of relatives, considered his besetting weakness was a kind of idle and lazy carelessness — a mental slovenliness, nearly connected with a continual desire to lie on a sofa with the eyes closed. When he went to Harrow and was in the lowest form, they said it was so characteristic of him. When he managed to get into "the sixth," they said, if he had not been so lazy he might have been captain of the school. Again, when he went up to Oxford and got a first in "Mods" and a second in "Greats," they said, feeling that they were only speaking for his ultimate good, "How easy 'Mods' must be, if dear Claud got a first! Indeed we're told that it is almost impossible to take a less distinguished degree than he has done."

Having left Oxford, he found himself at twenty-five called to the Bar without any immediate prospect of briefs. What could be therefore more natural than to find him called also towards the sunshine and the South? especially as

he had the greatest inducement of all—a pleasant
companion. For an old friend of his, Lord Darlington, who had once been his fag at school, and was
now a frank ingenuous youth—ladies called him a
pretty boy—of twenty-one, was with him. He was
tall and slim, with a small aristocratic head, blue
eyes, and plenty of light wavy hair, that had a habit
of tumbling over his forehead as though to assert
its individuality. No one had ever accused him of
being unwholesomely or uncomfortably clever; on
the contrary, he was delightfully simple and confiding. "Amiable" would be the word exactly to
describe him, if it were not already dedicated to
the process of "damning a friend with faint praise."
And faint praise (even when unaccompanied by
anything worse) would be quite inadequate to give
an impression of Darlington's character—a pleasant,
lovable character, that could be known and liked
at once, without any tantalising complications
which might interest one as a critic while alien-
ating one as a friend; or unknown depths of disposition (either brilliant or portentous), among
which one might suddenly find one's self left
doubting and in the dark.

It must not be inferred that Claud Brownlow and Darlington were the only occupants of the carriage, for at the other end of it were three other people : Mr Leonardo Leo, a celebrated critic, poet, and musician; and Mrs Leo, who was a no less celebrated beauty, completing what they would probably call "the harmonised circle of their existence" by painting dreamy pictures or "tone movements," formless, but redolent with colour, as her friends appreciatively whispered of them.

The Leos, however, were not merely what is commonly and vulgarly known as æsthetic. They were something much rarer and higher than this. They were broadly eclectic, deeply cultured, and (imagined themselves) extremely Hellenic.

Their home in town was so hushed and darkened, so guarded and beautified—its atmosphere, as it were, was so rarefied by the highest and most exquisitely exclusive culture—that profane people had been known, after a short time, to be seized with a brutal desire to scream, or otherwise assert themselves. It is even said that once a visitor in desperation did worse, and defiantly announced that Dickens was his favourite author, and Mozart the only composer he cared to listen to.

But Mr Leo was energetic as well as pictorial. He edited a review called ' The Highest Aim,' which was equally divided between literature, art, politics, and society. He was an ardent Radical of the " academic school," and looked eagerly forward to the time when a universal suffrage (including, as his wife said, " the stronger but unrepresented sex") would give the world an ideal government of perfect enlightenment, advancement, and justice ; and when the highest literature, the noblest art, the best government, and the most brilliant and exclusive society, would not only be common, but entirely universal. As he himself said—" The time when every working man will be able to join the Arundel Society, subscribe to classical concerts, read the best literature, and join with other working men in entirely governing the country, and taking their just share of the unearned increment of the rich, is still (with the exception of the last) a long way off. But when every man has been raised to this ideal position (the poor man and the rich man alike raised from their respective poverty and riches to a happy state of modest comfort) by universal suffrage and radical legislation, what a vast and astounding progression will have been made from our present tentative and imperfect condition!"

The fifth passenger in the carriage was the great Mr Giles. I say great, because, although he was as yet unknown to fame, beyond a moderate but ever enlarging circle of friends (and shall we whisper, victims?), he was one of the most powerful men in England.

If one wished to describe his position by using an elaborate metaphor, such as is sometimes employed in a sermon to bring home a vital truth to the congregation, one might point out how the passengers on an Atlantic steamer, as it steams forth in its beauty and elaborate perfection, hear the captain give his orders, talk to him, obey him, and know that he is in command, and is responsible for their safety. They give no thought to the immeasurable force that carries them onward, and which alone prevents them from rolling, helpless and forlorn, among the ocean billows. They laugh, and dance, and sing, and try to engage the captain in conversation, in order to show that they are on

terms of acquaintanceship with constituted authority; while far below them is a man, unseen, unknown, almost unthought of, who guides their vast
momentum with his hand, driving them onward,
onward towards the distant shore they cannot see,
where the calm harbour invites them, and the cruel
waves roar round the rocks that guard it, await-
ing but the slightest mistake to destroy them
utterly and for ever.

So the Liberal party had their captain, their
leader; but below, out of sight, with his hand controlling the machinery, was Mr Giles. He was the
President of the Centralised Executive Committee
of the Representative Hundreds of the party all over
the country. And if the Hundreds were a kind of
informal Parliament, the Executive Committee was
certainly an informal Cabinet, and Mr Giles an
informal prime minister—like the holder of many
other informal positions, having all the more power
because his right to it was unrecognised.

When he received what he called his "tip" from
the Cabinet, or the advanced portion of it with
whom he was in more immediate communication
(though even with regard to this he had been

known to carry out the Scriptural text, that it is more blessed to give than to receive), no Roman emperor was ever more autocratic than he.

The word went forth: the Centralised Committee were unanimous; the Hundreds agreed, and clamoured, and demanded; public opinion was triumphantly manufactured; and the Cabinet were induced to bring in, and enabled to pass, by the united voice of a great people, measures that caused the very men who passed them to feel some doubt, some apprehension—and that surprised, alarmed, and alienated the great majority of thoughtful and educated men of either party.

"But then thoughtful and educated men, from a merely voting point of view, are numerically worthless; and therefore their opinion need not be taken into account," said Mr Giles.

This was in reply to a remark of Claud's, and he now followed it up with a question.

"Then you do not fear," he asked, "that you will drive all the upper and 'propertied' classes over to the opposite camp?

"Not a bit. The Whigs will stay with us long enough to play our game; and when they have all

gone—they are gradually going over even now—
we shall have perfected our machinery sufficiently
to crush any opposition. I myself expect the day
will soon arrive—as you suggested—when nearly
all the well-to-do people will have left us. But
I don't dread it; on the contrary, we shall not then
be so hampered as we are now. Once let the
people get the idea it is a question of the upper
classes against the lower — the rich against the
poor—and we are made. We shall then perman-
ently secure a sufficiently large majority to enable
us to carry out our pet schemes for the future: a
graduated income-tax—with, I hope, a very steep
gradient — the land relieved from the landlords,
peasant proprietors, and so on. You know all
about it."

"I entirely disagree with you," said Mr Leo. "I
think that when the whole people have the vote—
especially after we have obtained female suffrage—
all class prejudice, class selfishness, and class interest will disappear. I think that the whole
people will not be less, but will be more just; and
I am quite sure that they will tolerate no economic
fallacies."

" They intend to have more of this world's goods than they have at present," rejoined Mr Giles. " I don't know about economic fallacies; but what I do know is, that if they were fools enough not to want more than they have, we should show 'em the way."

"But surely," put in Mr Leo, "unless it were conducted on strictly equitable principles, it would simply become bribery on your part, robbery on theirs."

" Oh no. The State can't rob—that's our latest principle. You don't call taxation robbery. Well, we shall simply arrange our taxation on a new plan. What you call robbery, we shall simply call the debt that the State owes to its poorest members. Or—or—well, the restitution of that unearned increment which the rich have stolen from the community. Bless you! when the time comes we shall have the names."

Mr Leo did not like the tone of Mr Giles's remarks. He thought they were a little too much flavoured with opportunism. Being himself, as we have said before, an academic Radical, with transcendental ideas on politics—acquired partly by

a study of classical philosophy and politics, partly
by an exquisite sense of the ordered progress of the
universe, modelling the British constitution, as it
advanced, into conformity with its laws—he felt that
there was something higher than a party platform,
or even a party cry; and that as the Radical
party—the party of progress—were acting consis-
tently with the laws of evolution, and were therefore scientifically right, and must ultimately pre-
vail, it was all the less necessary to bolster them
up with party dodges of a questionable character.
He suggested that to interfere with contract, for
instance, had been long ago proved to be both
useless and economically dangerous.

"Why, sir," said Mr Giles, "you must belong to
the *laissez faire* school. I didn't know that there
were any of 'em left. They went out when we
found that political economy wouldn't suit."

"We may not yet have discovered the true laws
of political economy," said Mr Leo, in his slow
deliberate way, while his "Oxford voice" enun-
ciated every word with extreme distinctness; "but
they exist, nevertheless, and are as unalterable
and as certain in their operation as the laws of

science themselves. You cannot evade or set at
defiance the laws of political economy without
injury to yourself, unless you can alter them by
altering human nature itself. Though after all,"
he added, more briskly, "I am not without hope
that we may be able to alter human nature a little
in the course of time; for I have no doubt that,
like everything else, it tends to adapt itself to its
environment."

"It will be rather uncomfortable if it doesn't,"
said Mr Giles. "Why, don't you know, not only
have our party given up political economy—sent
it to Satan or somewhere—free contract, unlimited
competition, and *laissez faire*, but we've given up
philosophical and scientific Radicalism also. All
that depends on the teaching of Herbert Spencer
and Darwin, and that lot. We don't intend to stand
the tyranny of Science; and as for 'fundamental
laws,' we don't like 'em. For instance, we don't
approve of the 'extinction of the least fit'——"

"Extinction of the least fit! I should think
not, indeed! Why, where would our future rulers
be then ?" put in Claud rather neatly.

Mr Leo was a little pained at Giles's tone. He

had, however, long considered that people of his class were useful in working the machine—with an extended franchise there is room for much machinery (of the more *useful* but less ornamental sort), and some one must work it—but that the great principles of the party should be left to be formulated by its higher minds. He therefore contented himself by saying—

"Well, well, we mustn't set the laws of science at defiance, you know. Even if religion ceases to influence us, we must still maintain a code of ethics and morality. We must remember that fundamental justice——"

"Fundamental justice now," said Mr Giles, catching at a phrase that he understood; "I don't know so much about that."

"Not very much, I think," suggested Claud.

"I don't go in for the philosophy of the thing, but I know what we want and mean to have. Why, I've got a friend in the Cabinet—I mustn't mention names—Cabinet secrets, you know. Well, he just gives me the tip, or we fix together what we want, and then I just send it round to 'the Hundreds'; and they want it—they de.

mand it unanimously—the members submit—the Cabinet wavers and gives in — and there you are!"

"I have often thought," said Claud, "that your party play with edged tools. They nurse their dangerous ideas as one might a litter of young wolves. 'They are so pretty,' one might say, 'so harmless—dear little things—just like pups!' But the day comes at last when you wake to find them a ravening pack of wolves. Then you fly, when too late, and you have to throw them one thing after another—you know the Russian story—till at last the driver has to fling himself to them in order to save his mistress and her family, whom he is driving. Though I admit," added Claud, with the lightest touch of satire in his voice, "there the analogy would most probably cease, as in *your case* the driver no doubt would throw over his passengers in order to save himself."

"I don't fear the wolves," said Mr Giles. "Why, if there are any—which, mind you, I don't admit —I'm one of them myself."

"You admit it," cried Claud.

"Well, you see, I'm not ravenous at present; I'm

only a pretty pup," said Giles, with a disagreeable laugh.

"You overlook and ignore, I think, that remarkable sense of political morality with which the English people——" began Mr Leo.

Only to be interrupted by Giles. "I don't want to argue," he said; "I don't argue—at least that's not my line. I haven't to gild the pill, or cover up the powder with jam—the Cabinet must do that; but what I have to do is to cram it down the patient's throat and make him swallow it."

The conversation here dropped. Mr Leo began to write an article for 'The Highest Aim,' on "The Unexpectedness of Political Emotion." He occasionally, however, leant forward to translate a word for Mrs Leo, who was reading alternately 'Charlot' and Rénan's 'Le Prêtre de Némi,' with a view to an article on the spirit of contemporary French literature which she was going to write for one of the magazines.

Darlington had not joined in the discussion, but had contented himself with murmuring "brute" under his breath once or twice when Mr Giles was speaking. He had long held that no repartee to an

argument you do not like is so crushing as a few
strong terms, judiciously applied in the interjec-
tionary manner. This method of treating a subject
is particularly convenient to those classes who do
not so much acquire their ideas, as inherit them ;
and who believe that the assignment of a reason
in support of them is tantamount to admitting that
the point in question itself is open to argument.
It may be noticed in society that such words as
" beast " and " robbery," purred through aristocratic
lips, are considered to effectually settle and disarm
the objectionable person or thing respectively ;
while among other classes there are many party
cries—such as " free trade," for instance—which are
considered to be so far above discussion that we
are never gratified by hearing a single argument
in their favour.

Darlington contented himself with requesting
Claud not to speak to "that creature" again.

"I am sure," he added, "that your uncle can't
swallow that cad."

Claud's uncle, Lord St Kevan, was a powerful
Whig, who had held Cabinet office, but had somehow been omitted from the Government that was

" in " at the present moment. He still, however,
believed that the future of his party would be as
glorious as its past; and he regarded people like Mr
Giles as useful agents, evolved by changing circumstances and advancing times in order to uphold
the continued supremacy of his class. For he was
a great Whig magnate. Next to the Throne and
the Constitution, he centred his creed in the great
families of the Revolution. He held the traditions
of Grey, Melbourne, Palmerston, and Russell, and
he endeavoured to carry out what he believed
would have been their policy. He was still reel-
ing, under the discovery that a Liberal Cabinet
might not only contain but even be controlled by
" new men." At Brooks's he sat about mysteri-
ously in corners with other old peers, and shook his
head, and planned diplomatic arrangements, acute
political combinations, and high political policy.
Whenever he thought the Radicals were getting
too strong, for instance, he would propose that
a Coalition Government should be formed. But
though the chiefs of his party listened to him
deferentially, as being one of the most influential
and authoritative of his order, they seldom acted

on his advice; for in these levelling days the "rank
and file" of a party have to be considered, and even
the wishes of the constituencies themselves must
to some extent be taken into account. He was, it
is true, alarmed; but he had not capitulated. He
still looked upon *polities* as a game in which he
and his order naturally commanded, both for their
country's benefit and for their own—*party government* (with its ministers, members, voters, its whole
machinery indeed) being the means by which that
game might be played.

But if the government of his country was slip-
ping from his grasp, he intended at least to be
absolute in his own family. The *patria potestas*
should still be felt by his *gens*. It filled him with
horror and indignation that Claud should have
become a Conservative. He regarded it as unnatural, unbearable, and inexplicable. The county
seat—he still had a county seat, which had always
returned a Liberal, and now that the agricultural
labourer was enfranchised, was safer than ever,—
this county seat, which he had long been nursing
for Claud, should now go to a distant cousin. He
even hinted that it would be as well if Claud re-

membered that he was a younger nephew (the title
descended to Claud's elder brother — Lord St
Kevan having no children), and treated the Bar accordingly a little more as though it were a ladder,
a little less as though it were horizontal and
merely a suitable instrument to enable young men
to pass their time pleasantly.

Claud was trying to explain all this to Darlington, when Mrs Leo looked up. The son of a peer
was "the son of a peer" even to this advanced and
cultured lady. She thought that the moment had
come when an acquaintanceship should be made;
and so, to make a beginning, she asked Darlington
what he was reading. When he told her it was
'David Copperfield,' she felt that the time had arrived for her to try and raise his mental tone. So
she replied (for it must be whispered that some of this
lady's detractors said she was utterly devoid of tact):

"Dickens! Ah! neither I nor my husband are
able to read him. I try; but I can't. I know
that my taste deprives me of a great pleasure; but
he seems so vulgar, so coarse. His pathos is sick-
ening; his fun is worse—it is cockneyfied, Philis-
tine, painfully insular."

"What novels do you read?" asked Darlington, in an awestruck voice. For he had never met any one so intellectually exclusive in his life before; and though his alarm of her was mitigated by the fact that he noticed her clothes did not fit in the least (they had grown in the ultra-æsthetic school), he still felt oppressed by her conscious superiority.

"Very few modern novels, except the best French ones. Of course I read all of those. But I can hardly bear any English novels except Howell's. All the others seem to me to be so crude. One always has the feeling that any moment one may come across a sporting scene, or something even more degrading—something that hints at stables and grooms, and coverts and race-courses. English authors don't treat their characters with his delicate and exhaustive analysis, and they generally have too much plot to make the book worth reading."

"Then you don't care for horses?" said Darlington, inconsequently.

"Yes, in their proper place—in a carriage, not in a book. But as I said before, I haven't much time for novels, because I am busy over a little work of

my own—a subject I have long taken an interest
in.   It is an essay on the comparison between
Hellenic morality and the morality of the middle
ages, as exemplified by the lives of the Medici
family and the Borgias."

"Dear me!" said Darlington, with opening eyes.
"They did some rum things, didn't they?"

"It is a very painful subject," replied Mrs Leo,
in her soft, deep, uninflexional voice.   "And if it
had not been for a strong sense of duty, a desire to
purify and clarify our culture from all sanguine
and misleading belief in the moral virtue of the
ages I have treated, I should not have ventured
to undertake it."   Then there was a pause in the
conversation, and the only sound in the carriage
was that of the train which was bearing them on
towards Nice.

CHAPTER III.

A FEW nights after this the weather was warm enough at Pompeii to permit of the dinner being served out of doors.

The red glow to the westward still lingered. Soft yellows and nameless greens melted while they rose upward in the sky—upward till they seemed to turn into a tender echo of the liquid blue in the east, now changing every moment to the radiant darkness of a Southern night. Here and there a star gleamed out like a drop of fire, as the light faded back from the gathering flush of deepening colour that shone in the wings of the evening, already folded over the dying day.

Black shadows lurked among the pillars in the Forum, and shrouded the mysterious vistas between them in brooding gloom. But here and there an electric light made a brilliant point of fire among the marbles; and the whole air towards the seaside was filled with a subdued glow from hundreds of wax candles, that lit the numerous little tables standing around.

At one of them Darlington and Claud were seated with two other men—Jack de Barry, and a would-be social comet who was just rising on the fashionable horizon, named Hugh Flashington. He was a tall, good-looking, extremely active young man, with an effusive manner, and an affectionate greeting for everybody. He was very clever in his way, and extremely quick at assimilating other people's ideas, and reproducing them as though they were his own. He aimed at being thought dashing, brilliant, universal—a kind of modern Alcibiades, or at least a Count d'Orsay—and considered that every one was to be "taken in" if you only "took them by storm" with a sufficient battery of eloquence and diplomacy.

Perhaps he had not the amount required, for he had never been wholly successful. People sometimes found out that the truth was often in absolute opposition to his statements; and while some

were dazzled, others were more than doubtful, even
coupling the ugly word "humbug" with his name.
But if he wooed admiration by some doubtful means,
every one admitted that he was a pleasant companion, and would prove an addition to any table.

The whole party were now nearing the close of
a suitable little dinner, and the conversation, which
had been fitful at first, seemed at last gradually
taking the place of a somewhat silent admiration of
the night and its surroundings.

"It reminds one a little of the piazza at Venice
in the evening," said Darlington, helping himself to
ice-pudding as he spoke; "only it's more—more
like a dream, you know."

"Don't you feel as though we were all in a grand
opera, just waiting for the curtain to rise?" replied
Claud. "If it wasn't for us people in trousers, it
might be a picture of Alma Tadema's come to life.
Just look at that servant, for instance;" and he
indicated a beautiful Italian youth, whose slim and
graceful figure was only protected by a short clinging tunic of Indian silk, below which his well-
made legs asserted themselves with classical independence.

"Yes; he is not a bad-looking fellow," said Darlington. "And they've invented a good airy costume for him, which must be very comfortable as long as it's hot and doesn't rain. But fancy him in a thunder-storm, with little streams of water running down each of his bare legs."

De Barry looked up. He was on the Committee, and had never approved of the artistic servants. He had wished, on the contrary, to import a number from the London club, who would behave and be dressed according to the strictest English idea of what is suitable. He therefore announced, with a little air of triumph, that the Italians' looks were better than their honesty, and that Smythe had had to give six of them warning that very morning for stealing spoons. "We have now telegraphed to London for some good club waiters. I shan't feel comfortable till I'm waited upon by a man in shoes and knee-breeches, who has had his hair properly done. Any one would fancy, if they turned up here, that we had left civilisation completely behind us."

"But it is so—so picturesque," said Claud.

"We don't want to be too picturesque," said De Barry. "Why, some wine was actually brought me the other day by a creature with a moustache. It's hardly—hardly decent. We may be playing at being Romans, but at any rate we are not savages."

"Of course," said Claud, "we are only playing at being Romans; but how charming it would be if one could really wake up and suddenly find one's self living eighteen hundred years ago! Only think," he continued, as a hundred classical advantages seemed to crowd themselves forward in his mind, "no dentists, and what is better—no need of dentists, no competitive examinations, nothing to ruin one's health and spirits. There would be no top hats, tight boots, or tailor's bills—none of our modern life, which sickens us with *ennui* if we pause, and maddens us with unhealthy excitement if we rush onward in its front. Fancy a free natural existence, when no one asked 'if life were worth living,' when one hadn't to be intellectual and enlightened, when no one had crotchets, and everybody did not struggle to be fashionable. We haven't slaves nowadays, but I bet we have thousands of people who would be only too glad to be slaves if their masters would keep them from starvation."

"But there would be no clubs, no operas," said De Barry. "Have you considered that there was no food fit to eat—not even a French cook—and certainly no wine that one could possibly drink? How could one live a day without railways, telegraphs, and newspapers? Where would be the country houses, the yachts, the everything that one requires—requires to keep one even alive?" (He did not exactly stammer, but he spoke with a certain delicate hesitation, a sort of catch of horror in his voice.) "I don't believe their society was even select. I don't believe you always knew who it was you knew, you know."

Flashington had been waiting for an opportunity to give his views, which were spoken as they were created, and were given to his friends in the form of a pleasant stream of discursive chatter.

"Think of the suppers! How one would have reclined, after a warm bath, on a couch, wrapped in a soft cool garment, and crowned with flowers. Something like being in a glorified Turkish bath. There would be philosophers to talk and improve our minds, beautiful slaves to wait on us, and flute-players, and all that sort of thing. We should have

parties like the one in Plato's 'Symposium'; and
some people would get rather excited with the wine,
and then we should all talk about love, and death,
and immortality, and politics, and scandal. Oh, *what*
scandals they must have had in those days to talk
about! Doesn't some one say somewhere that the
suppers were like the 'wines' one has at college,
only much more charming? I wonder if they were.
And yet I think, on the whole, I prefer our modern
ones; for at any rate we have 'fiz' and cards. I
think one *must* have cards. To have nothing on but
a cloak wrapped round you may be very poetic, but
I prefer clothes that have some 'cut' about them—
something to show that they come from a good
tailor."

Darlington was neutral, having a pleasant sense
that the present age is a very nice one, and that
one generally managed to enjoy one's self wherever
one was.

"Well," he said, "one gets plenty of fun out of
things now, and I suppose one would have got
plenty of fun then. If they had no cards, it didn't
prevent them from gambling; and that's the great
thing, after all. There was plenty of fighting. I

should have gone off to Britain on a grand tour. Nowadays every one knows everything about everywhere."

"Yes; and one could have had plenty of slaves," said Flashington, still wavering between the list of ancient and modern dissipations that was offered to him. "Why don't they revive the fashion of having slaves? If only some smart person would begin it, I am sure we could soon get the laws altered. I wonder if we shall ever have gladiators in the Albert Hall? It is such a pity that place should be so wasted; and the old arena must have been so exciting! I should have sat and looked on, while Claud—Claud would probably have been a persecuted Christian—was fighting with the wild beasts."

"You would certainly have been on the side of comfort and persecution," said Claud.

"Oh! I suppose I should have been a pagan," said Flashington, "before Constantine's time, or whoever it was who invented Christianity, — I mean, who invented it as an established religion that one could belong to."

"I wish we could persecute troublesome people

nowadays," said De Barry, looking up at a neigh-
bouring hill, where there were already signs of a
gigantic hotel in course of construction. "Just look
there! Stoker, the great excursion man, has bought
that hill, and is building a beastly great hotel to
overlook this place. There's a nice prospect! We
shall have three hundred brutes looking at us all
day through opera glasses, just as though we were
an exhibition; and the club will be ruined!"

"Let's go and 'rag' them," said Darlington.

But Flashington's extreme ingenuity in turning
everything to his own advantage suggested even a
better plan than this.

"Why shouldn't we throw open the club?" he
said. "Set up tables, and make it another Monte
Carlo. We could form a company, and be rich in
no time. It's so absurd paying subscriptions to
clubs instead of making money by them. Why,
long ago, when I was at Eton, I lost a lot of money
to a fellow in a bet. I got him elected to 'Pop,' and
he was so grateful that he quite forgot the debt."

The last faint glow left by the passing day had
now vanished, and the lights in the Forum shone
out all the brighter for the surrounding darkness.

Our party, having finished dinner, were smoking and sipping their coffee, with their chairs pushed a little back, while they looked round at the occupants of the other tables. Claud's eyes happened to rest on a party of three seated at one of them. A handsome lady, who was neither exactly young nor middle-aged—perhaps the phrase "well preserved" would best describe her; and an inane-looking youth, with a vapid expression, and an occasional giggle at (what appeared to be) his own jokes, were opposite to him; and facing them, with her back to Claud, sat a young lady, who leaned slightly forward, and seemed to be rather listening to the conversation of the others than joining in it. She had at least a charming back, Claud thought. And as she moved her head, the light touched the edges of her auburn hair with gold.

"Who is that youth?" asked Darlington, looking towards the party that Claud was watching.

"Don't you know?" said De Barry. "I thought every one knew him. He's Tottie Fobbes."

"He looks an insufferable little noodle."

"Most people dislike him; but most people know him—they say he's such fun. He was too

wise to put up for this club; but he has come out
with Lady Peterhouse, who is his aunt or something."

Tottie Fobbes was one of those people who could
only have been produced during the last third of
this century—a period which, if responsible for
the theory of "the survival of the fittest," seems in
practice to produce a larger supply than ever of
the least fit, who not only exist but flourish on
the very best that it has to offer. He had no mind,
no intellect, and apparently no soul. When people
said that he was "girlish-looking," they did not
mean that he was pretty, but only that his face,
being an utter negative, was sexless. There was
a tradition in his family that he had once learnt
to read and write (he had been too delicate, according to his mother, ever to go to school); but he seldom gave the world a chance of judging if this
theory was anything more than a polite tradition.
With no particular income of his own, and of
course quite incapable of earning one, he fluttered
about society, and lived on what is called "the fat
of the land"—partly provided by his friends, and
partly by confiding tradesmen; drew down the

blinds of his boudoir (boudoir being the only word which could adequately describe his sitting-room), and sat in the becoming light cast by pink shades over wax candles, while he entertained his friends at tea. He knew nothing but the latest scandal, which generally reappeared as the staple of his conversation in a deeply decorated and ominously heightened form. In fact, his power of making mischief was the only thing which prevented his being as contemptible as he was incapable, and which checked the pity one would otherwise feel for anything so effete.

"But who are the ladies?" asked Claud, still watching the movements of the little head that stood out so darkly against the candlelight on the table.

"That is Mrs Denbigh and her daughter. She— the mother—is rather a clever woman, and I suspect knows on which side her bread is buttered. The daughter is also clever, but is generally spoken of as being 'a strange girl'—chiefly, I should say, because she doesn't care much about the butter."

"She positively told me that she didn't care

about society, and that she preferred their place in Scotland to London in the season," said Flashington. "She is the sort of girl who suddenly asks you awkward questions. She once turned round to me at one of Lady Marlowe's evenings and said, 'Don't you think there is something a little contemptible about this? Here we are all priding ourselves on being superior people, because we have all been asked to meet one another.' Depend on it, she will marry an opera singer or a district visitor—some one whom she thinks is neglected by the world, but has a great soul."

"And what did you say?" asked Claud, a little impatiently.

"Oh, of course I took up the strain, and said what a good thing it would be if more people went as missionaries to feed the heathen."

Before Flashington had time to explain in what manner the heathen were to be fed by or with the missionaries, Darlington broke into the conversation, informing the others that she was a charming girl, could sing and dance capitally, and had all the right accomplishments for a young lady; but that, in addition to these, she could pull a boat, and fill cartridges, and make herself generally useful to a fellow, as he expressed it.

"And I suppose she can bait a hook," said De Barry.

"I don't know; I never asked her," said Darlington, innocently. "I daresay she fishes in the sea."

"When one goes sea-fishing with ladies," remarked Claud, "I generally find that one has to bait the hook, and pay out the line, and feel it to see if there is *really* a fish on, and pull it up again if there is, and then take the fish off the hook, and finally persuade the lady not to throw it back again into the sea, because she thinks it is so cruel to keep the fish out of the water, and its death-struggles are so dreadful. Then she looks round triumphantly and says, ' Oh, look what a fish I've caught!' "

"When ladies fish metaphorically, I don't find that they require an equal amount of aid," De Barry suggested.

"I have never seen a lady fishing metaphorically," Darlington said, by way of conclusion; "but I am going to speak to the Denbighs. Come, Claud," he

added, getting up slowly and throwing away the
end of his cigar; "if you like I will introduce
you."

Mrs Denbigh was charmed to see Darlington, and
asked him and Claud to sit down at her table.
Tottie, taking no notice of the interruption, continued an account of his exploits in a country
house that he had been lately staying at,—how,
when every one was in the drawing-room after
dinner, he had stolen a curled front from Mrs
Fitz Peter's bedroom, a "dress-improver" from
the room of another lady, as well as a dressing-
gown from Mr Fitz Peter's dressing-room; how,
arrayed in these, he had descended to the smoking-
room, and had been received with shouts of laughter. But he forgot to add that he had only just
escaped having his ears boxed by Mr Fitz Peter,
and that his host had politely informed him next
morning that there was a train to town at ten.

Claud was seated by Miss Denbigh, and only
gave a languid attention to these details; for he
was watching her face. Perhaps it was not round
and plump enough to be perfectly beautiful. It
seemed as though deep interests and high enthu-

siasms, a burning intellect and a restless spiritual energy, had refined the features and thinned the cheeks of everything that was superfluous to expression, and had left her soul free to shine forth through the almost transparent veil that it lit with its spirit. But if her face is not beautiful, he thought to himself, it is very interesting. It is better than beautiful; it is wonderful. It reminds one a little of some of Burne-Jones's paintings, only without the look they always have of dreary weariness.

At this moment the footlights on the stage at the end of the Forum were turned up. The Hungarian band in front of them began to tune up. There was a general rising from the tables, and every one began to take up the best positions they could find.

Mrs Denbigh rose. "They are going to play an opera bouffe—a company they have got over from Monte Carlo," she said.

Darlington, who loved comic opera, jumped up with alacrity, and the whole party moved off in the direction of the stage.

The piece was called 'La Princesse de Ravalenta

Arabica.' It was one of the latest examples of French comic opera, with the same conventional story that appears so often and in such very thin disguises—that begins in a village during the first act, meanders through the second act in a palace, only to vanish altogether in the third, before the arms (and legs) of young lady soldiers dressed in armour, and the limelight.

In the first act there was a rustic maiden (the programme called her "rustic"; but if the audience had depended on their eyes alone, it would not have been the adjective that suggested itself). She was betrothed to a young farmer; and, judging by the strains of the villagers, the curtain had had the felicity of rising on the very day when he was about to make her his bride.

No sooner, however, has the bride described her blushes in a waltz-song, than, in the midst of the "nuptial vows," horns are heard, pages enter, the centre of the stage is cleared, and the king of the country (played, of course, by the leading low comedian) enters, with a court of young ladies, who are attempting to play courtiers in hunting costume. He breaks into a long song, and describes how he has been driven forth from his throne by his usurping brother.

He at once enlists the sympathy of the simple maiden, and both he and his court are thereupon disguised as farm-labourers. Of course there is now a grand soprano chorus of farm-labourers, represented by young ladies in the ordinary farmyard costume of tights and spangles. The usurping brother (a fat man, with a deep voice and a rolling eye) having opportunely arrived at the fortunate moment when the chorus are beginning, is naturally charmed. He drinks with the virtuous maiden; he still drinks; he does not recognise his brother, who is standing by in the thinnest of disguises, and who is making the broadest of jokes at his expense. Soon he not only drinks, but is drunk. Then the simple maiden locks him up in a hay-loft. The king throws off his disguise and proclaims himself, the people cheer, the chorus shout, the principal characters shuffle up and down the stage in a line, the limelight is turned on, the country is saved, and the curtain falls on the first act.

Every one spent the interval between the acts in asking their neighbours what they thought of it.

Mrs Leo, who had condescended to be present, said she did not like it as well as ' Lohengrin,' and that, if people must play second-rate operas, she wondered that they did not choose something a little better—' Don Giovanni,' for instance. For it must be remarked that Mrs Leo's detractors accused her, not only of having no tact, but added (which is almost worse) that she was totally devoid of any sense of humour. Not that this in itself would necessarily prevent her from enjoying an opera bouffe—quite the contrary—but it often saved her from understanding jokes which other and less fortunate people are forced to laugh at, and it enabled her to take certain things seriously that the rest of the world can only see the comic side of.

On the other side of the Forum a group of men were standing round an extremely pretty girl, who was amusing them all with an account of a "mixed school" to which she had been sent in her youth. She was noticeably vivacious; her eyes sparkled, and little smiles chased one another across her face as she spoke. At this moment she was telling them how she and the boys used to "toboggan" downstairs on tea-trays.

"You're so stiff in England," she went on, in her unconventional and yet not unladylike way. "You don't get any fun. At least you do, but we don't —I mean the girls don't. Fancy having to be at school with one's own sex only. Why, I've never been alone with my own sex for a day, except when I went into retreat once for two days."

"Into retreat?" one of the gentlemen murmured.

"Yes. You mightn't guess it, but I'm very High Church, you know. It's more select, my mother says. But I didn't stay in that retreat long; it was just like a convent. Some of us sat all day and thought of our sins; but most of us sat and wished we had any sins to think of." Then with a sudden change in her voice—"Is that the second act beginning? I don't think I shall stay."

"Not stay!" cried several voices.

"No. I think it horrid," she said, with a grave look in her face for a moment. And then as though she feared its attributes might be discussed, she suddenly smiled again, and said, "I want to go a little walk instead, down by the sea. I want you, Mr Smythe, to be kind enough to take me, because I want to ask you all about the aristocracy. And

they say you are a great authority on their manners
and customs."

A slight smile went round the circle. Mr Smythe
was not certain whether this remark was prompted
by extreme ingenuousness, or whether its aim was
satirical; but he promptly offered the fair American his arm. And as she moved away from the
circle, her beautifully fitting Parisian dress making
the faintest rustle, and her little head standing out
in *piquant* shadow against her fluttering spangled
fan, she was heard to murmur to her companion,
" You really must teach me how to behave in the
English manner. I'm sure I say the most dreadful
things. And I may be a countess myself some day,
you know."

The second act of the opera (which was now
beginning) opens in the king's palace. The virtuous maiden is now a " court lady." Her lover is
depressed and discontented, as he has not risen
above being the shoeblack of the establishment.
The grand chamberlain is discontented—everybody
is discontented. There is a grand chorus of discontented pages, who suddenly cloak themselves, and
so become conspirators at once. The usurping

brother (having, it is presumed, slept off the effect
of the cider) most fortunately turns up at this very
moment.   Of course a grand conspiring chorus
must follow—when, in the midst of it, the simple
maiden rushes in.   She threatens to denounce
them; but the usurping *bass* tells her that he loves
her madly, and will marry her if she will only join
them.   This is too much for the light tenor person.
He rushes off and informs the king of the plot.
The conspirators are surprised, surrounded, and
every one suddenly, at the same moment, and
apparently from the same motive, bursts into a
wild dance of defiance, which continues till the
descent of the curtain obliterates it.

The third act, which appears to be weaker in plot
than in spectacle, opens in a camp.   The chorus of
young ladies reappear, dressed (perhaps if anything
a little less, rather than more) like soldiers.   The
virtuous maiden appears dressed as a soldier—so
does the weak tenor; and they break into a duet,
which is not interrupted by the evolutions of the
army behind them.   There is nothing to show who
is fighting against whom, or to whom the camp
belongs.   The plot has apparently come to an

untimely end (as is often the case in the last act
of comic operas); and in compensation, everybody
comes on in military dress, perhaps to finish up
the piece with military honours. Then there is a
chorus about nothing in particular; and all of a
sudden the simple maiden throws herself into the
arms of the light tenor, the usurping duke into
the arms of the simple maiden's mother, the king
into the arms of his wife, the soldiers into the
arms of the rustic maidens when there are any—
when there are none, into one another's—and (probably because the authors now think they have
fooled long enough) the curtain comes down, and
all is over.

At the end of the second act Miss Denbigh
had looked longingly out across the broad smooth
distances of water, here and there touched by a
sparkle as the foam which edged the little waves
was caught for a moment in the moonlight.

Her thoughts had wandered far across the sea,
to other climes and distant ages, vaguely mingling
with imagined pictures of the long-forgotten past.
For across these very seas the glad young Greeks
had sailed from their dear country—their sanguine

faces and ardent hearts overflowing with hope and
joy, and love and friendship, in the boyhood of the
world. Then the stern Roman came, with steadfast
eye and iron will. The dark and subtle Cartha-
ginian passed—and passed—and was no more.
Tall barbarians from the far grey North — fair
Normans with violet eyes and golden curls—swept
over the seas, conquering. But time went on;
and the ships which sailed to the golden East
carried gay Crusaders, fired by religion and filled
with adventurous delight, their dainty armour
glittering in the sunshine, and each with the
crimson cross of Christ upon his breast. And
then the waves bore northward the fiery Moor,
who brought from the sad desert his burning
crescent and his canvas home, nightly moving,
and yet none the less his loved abode. So passed
the centuries. Greek pirates, merchants, then noble
ships, and flying steamers came and went—still
come and go; while the waves and the sky change
ever, and yet alone are eternally the same.

Thus Miss Denbigh let her thoughts play lightly
among the centuries, until she suddenly recalled
Thackeray's ballad, " In the Bay of Biscay." And

at the remembrance of that most realistic epic of
the sea, she awoke from her dream with a little
laugh, and suggested that they should go out for
a row upon the 'sea.

Claud jumped up in a moment. Would they
come? he asked them. He did not think that Mrs
Denbigh would feel cold on the water, and he
should be delighted to give them a pull. Mrs
Denbigh felt inclined to go, but suggested that they
would want a *cox*; and Tottie being worse than useless in a boat, she evidently expected Darlington to
proffer his aid. But before either that young
gentleman could speak, or Claud had time to persuade them that no *cox* was necessary, Miss Denbigh assured them that she could and would *cox*.
A boat was soon found. Darlington and Tottie
strolled down to see them off, and to carry the
usual number of wraps. Tottie blew kisses after
them, and screamed out, "Take me in your boat,
love," as they gently floated away from the lighted
steps; and then he and Darlington went back to
see the third act of the opera.

CHAPTER IV.

AFTER the opera was over, Darlington looked vaguely round with the intention of finding some one to play pyramids with. But before he had succeeded in doing this, he was suddenly addressed from behind by a rather more than middle-aged young lady, with that peculiarly brisk manner and determined air which proclaim that their possessor has outlived her illusions. This lady nevertheless still had one left; for in her early youth she had heard some mistaken person call her very pretty, and she had ever since naturally laboured under the delusion that she was extremely beautiful. It was not a beauty to which she made any concessions, however,—she was too strong-minded for that. Her mechanically smooth dark hair was parted in the exact centre, and brushed with mathematical neatness on either side, away from what she would probably call her temples. Her dress, though neat, was constructed on strictly business-like principles, and her whole appearance was painfully neat and slightly forbidding. So that Darlington, as he looked at her, thought, " Here's a go ! "

" Excuse me," she said in a firm high voice; " Lord Darlington, I think. I really must introduce myself to you, I am such an old friend of your father's. My name is Miss Rattletubs. Perhaps your father has mentioned my name to you. He was kind enough to speak very highly of some little essays of mine on social subjects, called ' Jinglings of a Chatelaine.' "

Now she was one of those people who are called " strong-minded," not because their minds are particularly strong, but because they form an aggressive and unalterable opinion, immediately and for ever, upon every subject, small and great, entirely irrespective of their own knowledge or other people's feelings. And Darlington, who had no curiosity about eccentric human types and interesting varieties of personality, and who merely knew that he had never met such a person before, and hoped never to meet such a person again, was simply filled with a desire to get rid of her. He therefore murmured something that was intended as an acquiescence, and giggled a little to himself as he wondered what his "governor's" opinion of the lady must be.

But to Miss Rattletubs the conversation was only just beginning. "I saw in one of those horrid Society papers that your father was suffering from an attack of gout. I'm sure I don't know which of them it was. I hardly ever read them myself, and I'm told they contain the most dreadful scandals."

"One sees where one's friends are staying, you know."

"My friends are chiefly among the workers—the people who are trying to regenerate Society. They say that this sort of thing can't last much longer." Miss Rattletubs, like most of the people who are great at generalities, adopted the plan of frequently putting a "they say" at the beginning of her statements. "I am myself writing a series of letters to a brother about all this sort of thing from a worker's point of view. I hope to collect them and publish them under the title of 'Letters to a Brother, from a Sufferer in the South.'"

Now Darlington, who had been brought up among the upper classes, and who had never met a leading "intellectual worker," much less a live authoress, before in his life (if we except Mrs Leo), naturally felt somewhat awed and impressed. He thought, as we probably all do the first time we meet an authoress—"Dear me, I wonder if she'll put me in her next book. And if she does, whatever will she say about me?"

"I'm so busy with one scheme and another," Miss Rattletubs breathlessly continued; she was extremely "in earnest" about everything. She hated above all things what she called "luke-warmers," and was always taking up new schemes, (which ranged from "whole-meal bread" to "ribbon movements,") in order to regenerate mankind. "I've just started the pink and green ribbon movement. You wear the pink ribbon if you don't smoke between meals, the green if you don't smoke during meals, and both if you don't smoke at all. Now I think I can persuade you to try the green, at any rate."

"It's awfully kind of you. But, you know, I'm afraid I should look such a fool with it. Besides, you know" (and this was a happy thought), "it wouldn't be quite true, because I do sometimes smoke at meals." And then Darlington, looking round in a helpless way for a subject with which to make a conversational diversion, suddenly saw the young lady who had taken Mr Smythe for a walk. She was standing a little apart, talking with great vivacity to an elderly gentleman, and shading her face from the light with a big red fan covered with little twinkling spangles. She looked — standing there in a French dress, which, although extremely fashionably made, was a little *bizarre*—like a picture by one of the newest school of French painters; for she almost always represented "an effect," and formed the very beau ideal of an *impression*.

"Who is that girl—over there?" asked Darlington, bluntly.

"That Frenchy - looking girl? Oh, she's Miss van Knut, an American. And that's her father. He's immensely rich, they say. He got the contract for an overhead sewer in New York. It didn't somehow give general satisfaction, they say——"

"Perhaps it leaked on people's heads," put in Darlington.

"——And, I believe, has since been abandoned. But he made his 'pile' out of it. She's good-natured, but frivolous. I should think she has had no 'bringing-up' worth speaking of. And then she spoils her forehead with one of those 'idiot fringes.'"

"I thought everybody—most girls, I mean—had them."

"Not really nice girls—really simple nice girls. They used to be considered quite fast, and now they are so common and vulgar. The 'coming woman' won't have anything of that sort."

"Well, you see, the 'coming woman'—if she's coming—can't have come, so we needn't trouble about her," said Darlington, who was almost being irritated into epigram.

"There will soon be a very different sort of people. There won't be room for many stragglers in the fight of life much longer. I daresay you haven't ever thought about it, because you've probably been brought up at Eton and Oxford, or somewhere like that. They don't realise the tendency of the age, because they're almost played out themselves. They say that the Victoria University is quite taking the place of Oxford. And there's a school up in Yorkshire somewhere—I quite forget where—which, they say, will be better than Eton in a year or two,—the highest tone, and all the masters advanced thinkers."

"What a beastly hole, and what a brute of a woman!" thought Darlington.

His thoughts must be forgiven, as he did not give them utterance; and it must also be remembered that his vocabulary of abusive adjectives was not chosen with critical nicety, but was both limited and formed by careless usage. His contribution to a conversation was at all times more or less of a monosyllabic character, although atoned for by a charmingly responsive smile. Now, as he murmured something about Harrow being good enough for him, even the smile was wanting. Then he suddenly added, "I'm very sorry,—I must be off; some fellows are waiting for me;" and betook himself off accordingly.

Meanwhile the little boat was slowly floating seawards. Claud pulled as gently as he could; and finally, when they had got out about a quarter of a mile, he rested on his oars altogether. The conversation was taken up in fits and starts, and then dropped again, as though it were hardly worth while to talk when there was so much around to silently enjoy. At last, after a longer pause than usual, Claud pointed out to them Pompeii in the distance. It looked more lovely than usual this evening. The magic touch of the moonlight had removed every trace of newness and garishness. Lines of little twinkling stars marked the streets, and threw a hot faint light upon the pillars and porticoes of the classical houses and tiny temples among which they crept along.

"How much more beautiful it is now than by daylight!" said Miss Denbigh. "By daylight I think it all looks a little sham and tawdry, but now—why, even Venice can't be more lovely."

"Yes, it is a little like Venice — at least as Venice looks sometimes," said Claud. "Last time I was there, however, it was foggy, and raining the whole time. I had nothing to do but to stay in my hotel and read 'The Stones of Venice' and write sonnets to the weather."

"Do you write poetry much?" asked Mrs Den-

bigh, quickly. She thought to herself that it was
a pity when young men took to spending a great
deal of time in that way. If they were real poets,
perhaps it could not be helped, many things having to be excused and put up with in one of these
uncomfortable people. But, as a general rule, she
considered it should be discouraged. It had an
enervating effect on the character, and tended to
confuse the real issues of life with false standards
and misleading ideals.

Claud did not know what was passing through
her mind, and he answered, innocently enough,
"Oh no; never anything to be called poetry.
Sometimes, when I have nothing better to do, I try
to pump out some verses, just for practice; but you
may be sure I never bore my friends with them."

"We are quite sure of that," put in Mrs Denbigh,
with her ready tact. "But that need not prevent
you repeating some of them to us."

"Yes; please do," added Miss Denbigh.

Claud, of course, protested that he really
couldn't—that he would if he could, but that he
had really forgotten everything. He retreated
from one outpost of excuse to another, as a young

man generally does when he is pressed to do anything which makes him feel shy. And he sur-
rendered at last (as they generally do) with a
feeling of half-conscious pleasure after all.

"Well," he said, "the only thing I know is a
sonnet on the weather at Venice I told you about.
I sent it to the 'Spectator,' but they wouldn't put
it in. So I daresay it is very bad :—

> " Across the grey sea drifts the cold grey rain ;
> The palaces are veiled in grey ; and all
> The city seems as though a second fall
> Had driven forth mankind with sword of flame.
> St Mark's is masked in scaffolds, which proclaim
> Its downfall and its doom ; while Nature's pall,
> Deepening, descends. The campanile tall
> Towers in the mist. A wavering shadowy stain,
> Deserted, is the Grand Canal's wide stream :
> No boats among the bridges glide between :
> Even as of the dead, these waters seem.
> Ah no ! man is not dead. His latest scheme
> For joy in Venice comes. As in a dream,
> We see the passing steamboat's lurid gleam."

"Oh, I like it! I think it charming," said Mrs
Denbigh, when Claud had finished and had asked
her whether she did not think it a little pessimistic.
"But," she added, "why do you put in the word
'grey' three times in the first two lines?"

"Because the whole thing is a sort of arrangement in grey. The aspect of Venice changes daily. There is no place in the world which loses all colour so quickly when the weather is dull or wet. And, you know, there is no place which glows with such exquisite tints in certain hours of sunshine."

"Please don't tell me you paint as well as write poetry," Mrs Denbigh said, in playful alarm, "or we matter-of-fact people shall be quite afraid to know you."

"Oh no, I don't paint at all. Indeed I hardly ever write any poetry either. I'm fond of literature and everything else that is nice. But nowadays I am mostly taken up with my profession."

"And that is?"

"The Bar."

"But you are not at the Bar *now?*" suggested Mrs Denbigh, with the slightest touch of playful satire in her voice.

"Not at the present moment. I'm taking a little holiday." Then Mrs Denbigh gave him her views on the Bar as a profession. She was a clever woman, and her views on most subjects were not to be despised. She told him that she had often

met eminent lawyers in society during the course
of her life, and had also known many young men
in society who had adopted the Bar as a profession,
but they were never *the same.* And she suspected
that the eminent lawyers, when they were young
men, might have been found working ten or twelve
hours a-day in back chambers, up four or five
flights of stairs, somewhere in Lincoln's Inn.

She gave him her views with a certain insist-
ance, which made Claud wonder whether she
wished him to tell her his motives in choosing a
profession. He could not, however, state that he
was regarded as his uncle's heir, as far as a large
part of his personality went, so he contented himself by saying, " I went to the Bar chiefly to please
my uncle, Lord St Kevan. I think he considers it
a good step towards a political career."

Mrs Denbigh turned the conversation, — she
began to talk about Darlington, and filled Claud
with delight by praising him so generously. He
was such a satisfactory young man, so good to his
mother, and so popular in his county. He would
probably stand at the next election.

" Yes, I believe it is fixed," burst in Claud, " and

I am to go down and help him to kiss the babies, and all that sort of thing."

During this conversation Miss Denbigh had been very silent. Her thoughts had been far away— rambling over Scotch moors, wet with the falling mist and covered with watery bloom. Suddenly she said—

"I don't like 'smart people.'"

"Claudia!" said her mother.

"Well, perhaps it's the phrase I dislike. As far as I can tell, you may be well-born, good-looking, and well-bred; yet if you happen not to be in the 'smart set,' you are called second-rate. Whereas, on the other hand, you may be ugly, ill-bred, and rude; your father may have been a drunken money-lender or worse: but if you happen to have succeeded in wriggling yourself into the 'smart set,' you become a privileged person, and can look down on and snub every one else."

"But we are in the 'smart set,'" said Mrs Denbigh.

"I was only speaking about the general principle. It made me so indignant at dinner to hear Tottie Fobbes say, 'A fellow had the cheek to introduce me to Lord Mawnan. How can I possibly know him! He must be very second-rate, for I never meet him at any of the *best* houses.'"

"Yes, Tottie takes himself a little too seriously sometimes," said Mrs Denbigh. "You would never find a real man of the world—like Mr de Barry, for instance—talk like that."

"The idea," put in Claud, indignantly, "of a little insignificant creature like that presuming to patronise a man in Lord Mawnan's position, because he happens not to care to go to a few houses in which Tottie has managed to show himself! Why, Lord Mawnan is twice his age, has ten times his position, fifty times his experience, probably five hundred times his brains, and could kick him out of anywhere in no time."

Miss Denbigh flashed over Claud a smile of approval, and then said—

"You must admit that in society people consider that they belong to a privileged class. They may not use their privilege, but they consider that they have the right to do many things that they would not venture on if they were not in society — the right, for instance, of being extremely eccentric, or

overbearing, or capricious, or unbearably rude, to
people who are not in their set."

"Come, Claudia," said Mrs Denbigh, with the
slightest touch of warning in her voice, "you
must not be uncharitable; and you must also remember that all the best people are in society,
even if a few ill-bred people manage to clamber
into it, and misbehave themselves there."

She remembered the day—of course Claudia was
too young to do so—when she herself was not
quite, *quite* in the smartest set. And though she
had always been a woman of too much dignity,
and with too broad a view of the relative value
of things, ever positively to struggle or intrigue,
she had brought her diplomacy (of which she had
a large store) to bear upon any doubtful or anti-
pathetic forces, until she had perfectly gained her
end. Social position had never presented itself in
so crude a form as a ladder, but to her it had been
a gently inclined plane, up which she had enjoyed
moving.

After this accomplishment, she did not cherish
her conquest in proportion to the pains she had
spent in bringing it about (as most women—and,

indeed, many men—are found to do). In fact, she despised it a little in her heart. She quite sympathised with her daughter in her outburst; but she thought that lately her daughter had acquired strange socialistic ideas, and that they had better be checked as soon as possible. One of her hopes had long been that perhaps Darlington might propose for her hand. Mrs Denbigh not only liked him for his position, but also for himself; his charming face and frank boyish manner had a way of unconsciously insinuating themselves into most ladies' hearts. And now she wondered if Claud could be kept at a safe distance. All this, put down, perhaps a little crudely, in black and white, would lead one to suppose that Mrs Denbigh was merely an intriguing woman of the world. It was not really so, however. She had the kindest heart; and if she had her plans, what clever woman with few illusions, broad decided views, and a considerable natural power of getting them accepted, has not? She now, for instance, determined that they had been out long enough, and so the boat was turned towards the shore. As Claud was pulling them in, she asked him one or two more "leading questions" about his future career. Claud answered them, and then suddenly gave a little laugh.

"I am only laughing at my thoughts," he said, when Mrs Denbigh asked him if she were not horribly inquisitive.

The thought that had suddenly struck him as so ludicrous was the idea that Mrs Denbigh had absolutely taken alarm, and feared that he might fall in love with her daughter.

"How absurd women are," he said to himself, "to imagine such preposterous things!" And then he gave another little laugh, for at that moment the veil was lifted. He felt Love's golden arrow in his heart, as a blinding wave of seemingly mingling colour, music, incense, light, and bliss, swept over him. And he murmured to himself, "By Jove, I think she is right!" with a little rapturous flutter of perfect happiness.

CHAPTER V.

THE rain was pouring down. Dark clouds came sweeping over the tormented sea, scudding from the south, where their advent was lost in one obliterating sheet of grey pallor. The Forum was deserted; it was slowly transforming itself into a pool. Little streams of rain raced off the houses into the streets, and helped to swell the rivulet which each one had started on its own account.

The lashing wind blew in gusts, hurling the rain into the face of any one who was bold enough to venture, even with hurrying feet, from one building to another.

Most of the people were huddled together in one or other of the public rooms; but they were cold, and bored, and extremely cross. Many of the rooms themselves were not only damp, but were positively sloppy; and draughts, which in this case were violent gusts of wind, abounded.

Miss van Knut, after undergoing, as she herself said, the slow water-torture for some time—a drop of rain having fallen on her head every two minutes —proposed a warming game. Some one suggested a "tug of war," and the party were soon in the midst of England against the world.

"Have you heard that Cade is coming in a day or two?" said Mr Giles to Mr Leo, as they were standing watching the fun.

"Really, I shouldn't have thought this sort of thing was at all in his line. Is he interested in classical revivals?"

"No; but he likes enjoying himself as well as any one else. He is very fond of the good things of this life—very. He doesn't himself really hate the rich. He is only, rightly, envious of their privileges."

"Then his professing to do so is merely a policy?"

"Yes—part of his policy as a popular leader. You must do that sort of thing nowadays."

"But I always thought that as the Government became increasingly democratic, its leaders would also become more disinterested."

"It's no good being theoretical nowadays. You have to be practical if you want to succeed; and if you want to succeed in politics, you mustn't be too squeamish about the means. That's how Cade got on. You don't suppose he has risen to the Cabinet, from being a temperance lecturer, merely by patriotism and disinterested statesmanship! I believe that the chief reason he is coming here is to meet Courier, the great French Radical. I don't know much about him. I fancy he's not a bit stronger than Cade in his views. But the French have never let him get into their Government. They're so retrograde, after all. They are really much more reactionary than we are."

"Courier," said Mr Leo, in his gently authoritative manner, "is, I think, a very dangerous man. He is an unpractical dreamer—a Girondist. Like Rousseau, he believes that the ideal state is a state of nature, with apparently few laws, either civil or even moral. He thinks that if we obtained this state we should all be innocent and happy and beautiful—indeed ideally Hellenic. But here I, like most of the thinkers of the present day, differ from him. We must progress; we cannot retrace our steps."

"I'm afraid I must be off," said Mr Giles. "I
do the practical parts, you know, and I've a lot of
'wires' to send off to our Hundreds about autonomy for India. We're getting up public opinion
on that subject now. Cade's full of it, and I have
to work the machine for him."

"And I must be off, to read some of the 'Vita
Nuova' to my wife; so good-bye for the present."

"He's a rum chap," said Giles to himself, as Leo
walked away — "with his idealisms, and patriot-
isms, and laws of nature, and all that sort of unpractical wind-talk. Well, well, I suppose it all
helps the party; and it gives it a kind of pleasant
face, at any rate."

Lady Marlowe had provided a charming sitting-
room for herself. She had insisted on the architects giving her a good stove; and now she was, as
one might say, hugging herself over it with a certain satisfaction. The room was filled with photo-
graph-stands, Japanese screens, old bits of brocade,
and various other knick-knacks, which contrasted
strangely with the classically frescoed walls.

"Yes," she used to say, whenever Mr Leo sighed
over the anachronisms, "it is a jumble, I know; but

all modern art is. I'm going to have Sargent's
portrait of me put on an easel in that corner, and
then I'm sure the broadest eclecticism can't go
further than that."

Lady Marlowe was not, however, at the present
moment entertaining Mr Leo, for Mrs Denbigh
was seated on the other side of the stove, and had
come in to enjoy an "intimate" talk, as the French
say, about her daughter. Although well-born and
with an adequate income, Mrs Denbigh had always
found that a certain amount of enterprise was
necessary in order to maintain the very satisfactory position in which she found herself. But
Claudia did not realise this. To her the position,
with all the delights with which it was accompanied, came as a matter of course—as a dispen-
sation of nature; and she frankly accepted it as such.
Mrs Denbigh was really pleased at this. Nothing,
she would have considered, was a greater sign of
bad breeding than that her daughter should have
imagined that they were in any way privileged, or
that there was anything to be particularly gratified
at in their social position. And yet, although she
hated a worldly girl, she began to fear that perhaps

Claudia was getting a little too unworldly. Claudia thoroughly enjoyed and appreciated the good things of this life; but she preferred others still more. She would rather be hunting in Wiltshire during the winter than spending it on the Riviera, for instance; and she often bemoaned having to go up to London for the season, instead of enjoying herself, as she called it, in Scotland.

"If we could only miss a season or two, mother, no one would miss us, and we should have so much more fun in the country." Now Mrs Denbigh, though sure of the first statement, was not so sure of the second; and the whole idea filled her with a certain vague alarm. She thought that for a carefully brought-up girl—for her own daughter, in fact—the whole speech had a strange unnatural ring about it. Claudia had also taken to expending a great deal of time over "improving books." She not only puzzled out her Dante with the help of an Italian dictionary, but she had even begun to dip into Darwin and Herbert Spencer. Mrs Denbigh had the greatest belief in a woman being clever, intelligent, and well-read; but she drew the line at Herbert Spencer. So now she had come to have a little talk with Lady Marlowe, in order to discuss the great question of the idiosyncrasies and peculiarities of young girls in general, and those of her own daughter in particular.

"Claudia," she was saying, "is too much wrapped up in her own ideas. She sits and dreams all day over a book—not a novel, or even poetry, but social philosophy, or something of that sort. The other day I found her reading that awful 'Progress and Poverty'; but at any rate, I put a stop to that."

"Let her have more society and gaiety. Girls in the midst of pleasant action never retain theoretical ideas long. It is, after all, a form of enthusiasm; and when she is happily settled in life, her husband will take care that she isn't too transcendental. I'm sure Sir George never gives me a moment's peace to try and improve my mind. He seems to expect me to spend the whole day over the household accounts. If I am to do nothing else but look after the house, as I often say to him, what time is there to study esoteric Buddhism?"

"Oh, please don't talk to her about that!" said Mrs Denbigh, in alarm. "You can study such things and keep your head, because people like us, who have been in the world a little longer, know that it is all very pretty, but that it is only a passing fashion. But Claudia is carried away by what she reads and believes in; and I am now in daily terror of her suddenly announcing that she is a Buddhist, or a Theosophist, or a Socialist, or something dreadful."

Lady Marlowe, for her own part, thought that it would be both original and charming to have a daughter with "dreadful" views. Mrs Denbigh had a narrower ideal for a young lady. "Good form" (she did not call it by that name) was her criterion, and anything in the least original or *outré* she considered was most unladylike.

"If your daughter cares for politicians, I have got two coming in a day or two. Courier, the French Radical, and Cade — they want to meet one another, and so I asked them both here," said Lady Marlowe, taking a tack in the conversation.

"Cade coming *here* to stay with you! I always thought you were a Conservative; and even if you are a Liberal, how can you have anything to do with that dreadful man?"

"I'm a great Conservative; I'm on the Council
of the Primrose League. But for that very reason
I think it is politic to be friendly with the foe.
One can fight them so much better if one has
personally studied their weak points." (The real
reason that Lady Marlowe encouraged Mr Cade
was that he was very successful; and she wor-
shipped success, as a general rule, irrespective of
its merits or results.) "Besides, he is personally
quite a nice person; and one must always separate
the man from the politician."

"I have always considered him one of the worst
and wickedest people going," said Mrs Denbigh, in
her firmest accents—"not so much on account of
the nature of his acts, as on account of their wide-
spread influence. As far as this goes—and it goes
very far—it is tending to ruin the country; indeed
I daresay he will succeed in partly ruining it."

"Oh, come!" said Lady Marlowe, in her light
staccato way; "he isn't nearly so bad as you make
out. He is very good company, and I assure you
doesn't mean half that he says. We must try not
to be narrow-minded, you know, in this cosmo-
politan age."

Before Mrs Denbigh had had time to reply, a knock was heard at the door, and Flashington burst in. He had come, he said, to try and find Miss Denbigh. They were going to get up a four at lawn-tennis, as the weather had cleared up a little. Claudia was soon found in Mrs Denbigh's rooms. She and Flashington walked down to the courts together, which were already filling up, as ragged gleams of sunshine (with the sudden warmth that sunshine always seems to bring with it in the South) began to break through the clouds in glaring jagged rents, edging them, by contrast, with lines of crumpled darkness. The wind had dropped, the rain had ceased. "In half an hour," said Flashington, "it will have turned out quite a beautiful day. The court will be disengaged in a few minutes." And then he told her that the other two players he had asked were Darlington and Miss van Knut.

Darlington was already on the ground, looking more boyish than ever in his flannels. In a minute or two Miss van Knut was seen walking slowly towards them, swinging her racket, and dressed in a costume which here and there gave out a little

sparkle, as though the light in her eyes had overflowed and been deftly caught among its folds and
trimmings. Flashington introduced Darlington to
her. She flushed for a moment with pleasure,
and then said eagerly, but with the most absolute
simplicity—

"I'm so glad to meet you, Lord Darlington, because, do you know, I've never spoken to a real
peer before."

"But I'm not a peer," said Darlington, beginning
to get a little embarrassed—at the same time giving
her the winning smile with which he always carried
off his embarrassments so successfully.

"Then at any rate you're a legislator, and sit in
the House of Lords. I've been so carefully brought
up, that I've never been allowed to speak to a
legislator before. In America the high-toned
families don't generally associate with them."

"But I don't sit in the House of Lords; and I
hope it will be a long time before I do. They say
it's awfully dull there. I'm going to try and get
into the Commons next election."

"And of course you're a great Tory?"

"No, I'm a Liberal. All our family are, you know."

"You don't look as though you'd studied politics much. You look too young and too fresh, too——"

"Innocent," suggested Flashington.

"Yes, that sort of thing—too nice, in fact. Though I'm sure I oughtn't to say so. You should just see our politicians. They aren't too innocent or too nice. But how shall you know what to vote for?"

"The 'gov.' will tell me. Sometimes one's constituents have ideas on the subject. And then," added Darlington, in his most ingenuous and charmingly boyish way, "I've got some ideas of my own, you know."

At this moment Mr Smythe was seen deliberately approaching. He was a little short-sighted, and did not recognise any one as yet.

"I don't like that man," said Miss van Knut in a quick whisper. "I'm sure he's an awful snob. We have snobs in America, but we couldn't produce anything so perfect as that."

"That's why he's got on so well. They say he began life in a cheesemonger's. But our courts are ready now," added Flashington in a louder voice.

Mr Smythe now came up and gave the party a smile.

"We are going to play together," said Darlington to Miss van Knut.

"I think so; but I play so badly, you will have
to take all the balls," she said. And then turning
to Mr Smythe with a wicked twinkle in her eyes,
she added, "I shan't have to trouble you to give
me any more lessons in the deportment of the aristocracy, Mr Smythe, because Lord Darlington has
kindly promised to give them to me himself for the
future. Haven't you, Lord Darlington?"

"Rather," said Darlington with a delighted giggle,
as they took up their places for the game.

Mr Smythe, for once in his life, was staggered.
He was accustomed to put up with snubs and re-
buffs—at least from the right people. But he considered that he had never in his whole life met
with such a mixture of impudence and effrontery—
such a barefaced and shameless attempt to secure
a desirable young man, combined with such an
impudent snub for himself. He would have been
the last person to understand that such an idea as
"securing" Darlington had never entered Miss
van Knut's head; that the amount of amusement
she derived from a person was generally the test of

whether she wanted to know them well or not; and
that, with her frank simplicity of character, when
she liked any one she showed that she liked them
—indeed she was capable of even telling them so.
If she had thought that people would be inclined
to suspect her motives, she would at first have been
incredulous, and then indignant.

"I never heard anything so uncharitable and
horrid," she would have probably said, and at once
have gone and told Darlington that she could never
speak to him again.

"I must really go and warn some of the ladies,
and write to Darlington's mother at once," said Mr
Smythe to himself. "Dear Lady Downstreamdown
would never forgive me if anything fatal happened
to her son."

And Claud, where was Claud all this time? If
he were in love, why—even if he were left out
of the tennis set—was he not lingering round
the courts; or at least combining business with
pleasure, by giving Mrs Denbigh a little of his
company?

Claud at this moment was taking a long walk
by himself, up among the hills. He walked on

quickly. He told himself that he wanted to have a quiet time to think things over; but in reality he tried, by such mild violence as the exercise of walking gives, to escape from thought.

He was in love, and he knew it.

During the last few days he had moved, as it were, in an atmosphere lightened and rarefied by a new joy. He seemed to have been led away from the sordid world by the dreaming and passionate Love-god himself—the brows of the amorous boy crowned with myrtle, his grey eyes filled with a wistful exultation. Upwards and onwards they seemed to pass, till they almost floated among the peaks of virgin whiteness—in a world which we know not, fashioned as it is by lovers' hopes and dreams and whispers. And then, amid the rosy dawn-clouds, the young god spread his shimmering wings. And the air was filled with her presence— the presence of the one whom he loved. And her face smiled on him, while his blood danced through his veins, and he counted unconsciously the beating of his own exultant heart.

Everything around him was touched by change, was glorified and vivified, and, in a subtle way,

almost transformed for him—the small things of
life as well as the greater ones.

The flowers, for instance, that came with so fresh
a glow in the early morning—the distant strains of
music from the shore, almost too honey-like in their
sweet, long-drawn-out Italian melody—the faint
smell of orange-blossom that always pervaded the
place—the hills, the waves, the very people themselves, and the full-toned life around,—were partly
effaced, partly lit up by the luminous glow of his
love.

And yet he tried to evade the belief, and persuade himself that he was only possessed by a passing fancy.

During the last few days he had often waited
feverishly for hours with the hope of exchanging
a few words with her, or even getting a passing
smile; and then when the supreme moment came,
he found that he had nothing to say, or worse than
nothing. For words that did not rise to the occasion, he felt, simply mocked and insulted it.

They had had several small talks. He believed
they talked chiefly about the weather. And when
they had finished, he had cried to himself, "I am

not in love — I cannot be in love!" till the old irresistible, haunting, irrevocable feeling gathered over him once more.

Claud had a considerable amount of common-sense; and sometimes, when he was prepared to admit to himself that he was in love, his sense of humour even came to the surface, and helped to present a new series of pictures to his brain. He saw his uncle's look of wonder; he heard the sarcastic question as to how he proposed to support a wife. He heard Mrs Denbigh asking the same question with surprising clearness. But he did not hear himself giving an equally satisfactory reply.

"I can't marry, and that is the long and the short of it," he said to himself. He did not of course convince himself (does a lover ever do so?), but he continued, "I must cure myself. I'm in the most absurd state. I feel just like Dante when he wrote the 'Vita Nuova'; and, as Darlington would say, I never thought I should make such a beastly fool of myself as *that*."

He threw himself down on some grass which had been partly sheltered by overhanging trees from the storm of the morning; and then, slowly stretching out his legs, he gazed across the distance, beneath an arch of trellised vine, to the expanses of the sweeping sea. He lit his pipe. The afternoon was warm and very calm—his body was a little weary with its climb.

"I am in love," he said. And as he did so, he gave a tiny smile—and was asleep.

CHAPTER VI.

THE Government, at the time of which we are writing, although they might have lost a little of their originally overwhelming prestige, were still as firmly fixed in office as ever; and the Opposition saw no chance of either defeating them by a vote of censure, or of securing a majority if there were to be a dissolution.

It is true that there were ex-members of the Cabinet itself who said that it had committed robbery, condoned treason, and commanded murder.

The Ministry had forfeited one of these members by bringing in a bill which was simply a form of legalised theft; had forced another to retire, rather than encourage disloyalty and form compacts with traitors; and a third to resign when they began to bombard the port of a friendly Power without any declaration of war.

But so strange are the English people at times, that these little incidents hardly affected the popularity of the Cabinet—or what remained of it.

" Not until the whole Cabinet have resigned " (it is presumed through their distaste for assisting any longer in a Government of failure and disgrace) " shall we really know or realise the unequalled strength of the Prime Minister," some of his more devoted followers were wont to exclaim—and it really seemed as though the country agreed with them.

(The reader must remember, in justice to the novelist, that it is his business not only to describe, but also to create; and that therefore, if he mention, as though they were facts, things not merely contrary to all experience, but almost incredible in themselves, it should be ascribed to inexperience, and not be condemned as a childish attempt at deception. Indeed, is it wonderful that, when he has so often been told that " fact is stranger than fiction," he should have, for once, exceeded the credible, and made fiction stranger than fact ?)

After this, it will probably be impossible to astonish the reader—even when he is told that our (fictitious) Prime Minister was a Liberal, and is assured that Mr Cade was a member of our (supposititious) Cabinet.

At the present moment, Parliament had adjourned for the Easter recess, and thus Mr Cade was enabled to become a guest of Lady Marlowe's. Lord St Kevan had also arrived, and had shown by his manner to Claud that he had not yet forgiven his desertion. He was too magnanimous, too much the *grand seigneur*, to harbour any petty spite or to cease for a moment to be as exquisitely courteous as ever. But, on the other hand, he was accustomed to be obeyed, and now showed in his intercourse with Claud the very slightest shade of stiffness. His manners were very elaborate, and included many delicate shades among them—and he seemed to be waiting, with well-bred patience, for his nephew to rearrange his views, until they coincided with his own.

For a day or two neither of them touched on the dangerous topic. But one morning, when they were walking along the seashore, away from Pompeii, Lord St Kevan suddenly began, in his slow, deliberate, senatorial voice—

"I have been thinking over what you told me about your desire to change your principles" (he would not for a moment admit that his nephew could already have permitted the change to take place). "Do you not see that although there is much that is accomplished by a Liberal Government nowadays of which we cannot approve, yet if we, as an order, were to go over to the other side, things would probably become much worse? We should lose our controlling—our restraining—influence——"

"But you don't control—you can't restrain; that is just my point," broke in Claud—forgetting in his eagerness that his uncle had been born in days when peers were not accustomed to be interrupted, whatever they might say. "You allow the Radicals to outweigh the whole party, and then you throw your weight into their scale. Now, if you want to balance them, I think it would be more logical to throw it into the other one."

The old man seemed to take no notice of the interruption; and he continued, with his air of gentle dignity, as though Claud were still a child, and he were trying to convince him of an error, instead of punishing him for it—

" I think you underestimate the Whig influence. It would be impossible to form a Government without a large, I may say a preponderating, Whig element in it."

"At the present moment, possibly, but not for long," replied Claud, still unconvinced—still almost unabashed. "The Radicals openly scoff at the Whigs. You know they do. They say, if the Whigs choose to help them, well and good, but that they could do quite well without them— perhaps better; and that they will only accept their aid on condition that they—the Radicals—entirely control the policy of the Liberal party. The truth is, my dear uncle, that the Whigs like to think they drive the party. But they have let the reins slip through their fingers; and while a few have been left in the road altogether (to be picked up by the rival coach), the remainder are either being dragged or are pulling behind, in the vain hope that they may not be observed to be there. Mr Cade is really the coachman, with people under him, like Mr Giles, as ostlers, to do the dirty work."

"Metaphors are proverbially misleading. You probably know very little about the internal workings of the Government. We do, to a large extent, form the Government and control its actions. Without the Whig peers, with their influential and independent position, their business-like ability, their traditions of statesmanship, and inherited aptitude for government, the Liberal party could hardly exist, and could never come into power."

"I have noticed that although you so dislike my having become a Conservative, you yourself seem, to judge by your long and frequent letters to the 'Times,' to disapprove of the Liberal policy in detail, and to distrust almost all the Liberal measures."

"To a large extent I do, at the present moment. But I hold them to be an abnormal growth, due in a great measure to Mr Cade, who is, I think, a very dangerous person."

"Cade," broke in Claud, "I simply regard as an unscrupulous demagogue, who, for his own private advancement, is wilfully trying to break up his party; is violating every high tradition and un-

written law, not only of political morality, but even
of gentlemanly conduct itself; and is quite prepared,
if necessary, to assist in the ruin of his country,
which I, for my part, think will probably be one of
the most successful of his exploits—as party pas-
sion runs so high, that his party would probably
assist him to ruin his country rather than permit
him to destroy itself. They hate him, but they
obey him—because he knows his own mind, and
they don't know theirs. He takes a logical position, and they haven't one to take. He has petri-
fied them by his Jacobin machinery. And I think
that finally, by destroying the British Constitution,
he will succeed in becoming himself Prime Minister."

"We must be careful about our language, Claud.
But I agree with you that Mr Cade has too much
power. It is, however, I assure you, quite impossible that he could ever be Prime Minister."

"I don't see how you can prevent it; but we
shall see. Now what do you think of people like
Giles, for instance?"

"Such people are useful tools. I know that the
Conservative organisation is defective; but I suppose that even *you* have election agents?"

"Not like Giles. You will find that he is ceas-
ing to be a tool, and is gradually turning, with Cade's
help, into a dictator. And what about Ireland?"

"The misgovernment of Ireland has been deplorable—deplorable. But you must admit that both
parties are to blame for their lamentable and fatal
weakness. Mark this, Claud: whichever party you
may eventually belong to," said Lord St Kevan
solemnly, "it is *generally* fatal to a country when
it begins to persistently break the moral laws; but
it is *always* fatal to a country when it begins to persistently break the economic ones. I agree with
you entirely as to the Radicals having too much—
much too much—power at present. This seems to
me to be the very reason why we should *not* leave
our party — why, on the other hand, we should
bring all the power and influence and talent which
we may possess to bear upon our party for its true
good, and in so doing, support its constitutional
wing, by counteracting the socialistic part of it.
Why, for instance, at the present time, some of
the more moderate men of the Conservative
party might join us, and help to form a Coalition Ministry."

Lord St Kevan was a shrewd man; but he never realised that the days of Coalition Ministries are over, and that Cabinets are no longer formed, re-arranged, and dissolved by a few privileged gentle-men, in order to suit the will and pleasure of a dozen great families.

"Possibly, from the point of view of a great Whig peer, you may be right. But I, you see, am nobody. I don't affect any party by my change. And there-fore I think it right, as far as I have any influence, to give it to the party which I consider at the present moment is the most constitutional and patriotic."

"I suppose you already take part in the tom-foolery of the Primrose League?"

"Yes, I am a member. I think myself that in some ways it may be a little foolish; but *you* have enfranchised so many very foolish people, that it is necessary sometimes to stoop a little towards their level," replied Claud, with a momentary air of triumph. "At any rate, it is harmless. *We* only promise to uphold the Throne and Constitution—in this way differing, I admit, from the many mischiev-ous, dishonest, and ruinous promises which your party hold out as a bribe to attract their followers."

"I think we have discussed the subject enough," said Lord St Kevan, a little stiffly. They were entering Pompeii on their return. "I am lunching with Prince Chioggia, so I must say good-bye;" and he turned up a side street, leaving Claud to make his way alone to the central part of the town.

And so uncle and nephew separated. Really holding almost identical views on all fundamental questions, they only differed in their manner of approaching and their mode of expressing them.

Lord St Kevan in his heart admired Claud's quickness in divining the growing powerlessness of the Whigs, and was pleased at his generous indignation against the petty meanness, the unpatriotic partisanship, which were shown by so many members of his party, who violated their principles in order to retain their offices. He knew, with a sorrowful certainty, that no one had. the pluck to say to Cade, or even to a greater than Cade, "We draw the line here. We know that this policy is illiberal and unconstitutional; it is opposed to both moral and economic laws, and if persisted in, will be fatal to the country."

Claud on his part respected his uncle. He ad-

mired his steadfastness to all the inherited principles of his family. And he knew that, to his
uncle, the difference between the two parties was
as the difference between light and darkness.

"It is possible to do wrong in the light," his
uncle would probably say—"it is even possible to
do wrong in consequence of the light; but is that
any reason why we should leave the light for the
darkness?"

And yet between these two, both generous, and
each one trying to do justice to the other's point
of view, the great wall of party had grown up. To
a man in Lord St Kevan's position, with his training and principles, Claud's desertion was more than
an error—was only less than a crime. In his heart
of hearts he feared that the old order was passing
away; and he held that this was the very reason
why its children should stand by it till the last.
It was this that made desertion the more ignoble,
the more cowardly. There need be no decline if
all were faithful; but every desertion tended to
hasten the end, if the end were coming. So in the
midst of all his love for his nephew, he felt a
cold spot in his heart, and a sense of bitter dis-

appointment, almost of shame, took possession of him.

It is feared that a slightly erroneous impression may have been given of the place that politics occupied in Claud's thoughts and words; and that, judging from the specimens of his conversation which we have come across, it might be inferred that he was at all times a very serious and solemnly earnest person. No idea could be further from the truth. On a few subjects he thought deeply, felt strongly, and expressed himself decidedly, even eloquently, when they were touched upon. He nursed enthusiasms—almost romantic in their intensity—far down in his nature. But on the surface, no one could take light things more lightly or everyday affairs more easily. He combined, with a great deal of common-sense, a decided vein of humour. And these would have been sufficient to save him from ever tending to become priggish, even if his natural high spirits had enveloped less frivolity than they happily did. Besides, was he not in love? And who that is in love can give himself up to anything else?

At the present moment he was seated in the gig

of Lord Mawnan's yacht, with Mrs Denbigh and Claudia, Lady Marlowe, Mr Smythe, and the Leos. For Lord Mawnan, though not in what Tottie considered *the* smart set, and therefore not honoured by his acquaintanceship, had suddenly turned up in a charming hundred-ton schooner, The Shirt-front, which it appeared he possessed. He had asked some of his friends to come out to the yacht for lunch. He had a fancy for literary people, and had long known the Leos slightly. They, on the other hand, had long known him intimately; for to them a peer was still a peer, and they had not yet acquired Tottie's delicate perception of social differences. Besides having a fondness for literary people, Lord Mawnan had a special interest in Mrs Leo. He admired her beauty, and he delighted in plying her with playful banter.

Mr Smythe had managed to get himself invited by the same method that he employed to insert himself everywhere. Having in middle life emerged from comparative obscurity among the middle classes, he still proclaimed both the nature and place of his origin by indulging the world with his words slightly flavoured by a Somerset accent.

He had gradually managed, by perseverance, to make himself at first tolerated, and then even more or less necessary, to a large number of people. He was found to be very useful, and was used accordingly. The *jeunesse dorée* of the London clubs, indeed, made jokes and invented playful libels (in their heartless aristocratic way) at his expense. That he had begun life in a cheesemonger's shop was of course one of these; just as his having been a Mormon, and his having beaten a drum in the Salvation Army, were others. He good-naturedly forgave the youth (if they were very gilded), and they in return tolerated him; for he made up lists of young men, and supplied them to ladies who wanted a wholesale contingent ordered in for their dances.

There was a slight air of constraint over the whole party in the boat. Mr Smythe, for instance, was wondering why the Leos were asked, and whether he had made a mistake in not "taking them up." Were they going to be "coming people"? he asked himself. A keen instinct for coming people was part of the equipment of his profession. And could people be going to be so foolish as to make her a "beauty"? For in his

time he had sometimes seen fashion create beauty
out of much more unpropitious material than Mrs
Leo was composed of. Mrs Leo, on her part, did
not care to talk. She heartily despised fashionable
people. She believed that there was no one in the
boat who could appreciate anything she might care
to say; and she was quite sure that nothing they
could say would have any interest for her. For
some days she had been getting tired of Pompeii
itself. She tried to persuade her husband to take
her on to Sienna, " where they could be quiet." Mr
Leo, although fond of culture, and professing to
despise the world in general, was really rather
worldly at the bottom of his heart. He had no
desire to remove himself from a place " palpitating
with actuality and scintillating with fashion." Even
now he was trying to interest Mrs Denbigh by a
paradoxical conversation, half playful, half in earnest, and was assuring her that wisdom is extermin-
ated by education. She was, however, giving him
but half of her attention; for something—perhaps
the exquisitely acute maternal instinct which de-
velops itself in the mothers of Society whenever
danger threatens their daughters—seemed to warn

her to be on her guard. There were certain glances
in Claud's eyes, tones in his voice, that she did not
like. Claudia, she was sure, had noticed nothing as
yet. But it must be put a stop to at once and for
ever. Claudia was just the girl to take up a romantic idea and throw herself away—for she had a
certain gentle serious tenacity of purpose which
her mother dreaded. At the present moment her
mother knew she was simply enjoying the air which
blew in their faces so freshly, and the bounding
motion of the boat as it danced over the little
glancing waves.

By this time they were nearing the yacht. Lord
Mawnan's figure stood out darkly at the gangway,
waiting to welcome them. He was a sturdy well-
made man, about five-and-thirty, with a dark bright
face, and a closely cut black beard. He was
dressed in a loose yachting-suit of blue serge. He
was smiling and waving his hat. His whole manner and bearing seemed to radiate a breezy air of
health and wholesome prosperity. And as he stood
there, he was a picture of what a well-preserved
Englishman should be.

" Here you all are ! " he said, in his deep voice,

as the boat came up alongside. "Let me help you
up, Mrs Denbigh. It's awfully good of you to
come, Mrs Leo; we've no '*Botticellis*' for you on
board, only bottled stout. How are you, Smythe?
I hope I haven't torn you away from the
Princess Chioggia; or perhaps you've brought her
with you in your pocket—the last captured speci-
men, you know." All this was said in a cheery
voice, and with a good-humoured smile which
ought in itself to have disarmed offence, no matter
with what words it was accompanied.

The party were soon on the deck; and then, as
lunch was ready, they descended into the cabin.

"Mrs Denbigh must sit on one side of me, and
Mrs Leo on the other. Then, with Miss Denbigh
opposite, my cup of happiness will be overflowing,"
said Mawnan, as he arranged the company round
the table. "Smythe, where will you sit? I must
keep you in a good temper, or you will omit my name,
I know, from your next season's list of young men."

Smythe was touched in a tender point, but he
kept the smile on his countenance fixed, and said,
"I—I shall be delighted to put it down. I didn't
know you cared to go out."

"Well, 'pon my life, I don't think I do!" said Mawnan, cheerily. "One party's so like another."

"There are differences," suggested Smythe.

"Oh, I know there are—especially in the quality of the champagne," laughed Mawnan. Then he turned to Mrs Leo with a mischievous twinkle in his eyes—

"You know, Smythe gets up lists of all the suitable young men—I don't know if they pay him for the honour, I'm sure; and then a duchess sends for his lists, and orders in the men at the same time that she orders the supper."

"I can believe anything of young men nowadays," said Mrs Leo, in her cold deep voice. "Being brainless, they naturally take it as a matter of course that they should be ordered in like the plants."

"But they show their independence, I can tell you, by the coolness—some people would call it rudeness—of their behaviour after the invitation has arrived. For generally they either accept and then don't go, or they don't answer and then do go. And when they get to the party they only stay as long as it suits them, and refuse to dance if it's obvious that they're wanted to."

"I think that the only position more humiliating than theirs is that of the man who sends the invitations," said Mrs Leo, quite calmly.

Lord Mawnan felt she was going a little too far; so he said, "Oh, come now, you mustn't take it too seriously. I was only chaffing Smythe, you know; the lists are really very useful, and save a lot of trouble, I daresay."

Now Mrs Leo's strong point was not the reception of banter; and when she fancied that any one was trying to "draw her"—she was easily drawn—she at first became monosyllabic, and then extremely rude. She now turned on Mawnan.

"I dislike chaff," she said; "it is so frivolous."

"Aren't you ever tempted to be frivolous yourself?"

"I have few temptations, and that is certainly not one of them. If it were, I trust that I should have sufficient self-respect to overcome it."

"Dear, dear, how dull to have no temptations! I should think that a little chaff sometimes would act as a tonic, — would brace the system," said Mawnan, pleasantly.

Mr Smythe had been sitting in silent fury since Mrs Leo had snubbed him. He had made up his mind that now, at any rate, she should *not* be a beauty. At the present moment he could think of nothing more crushing than the inquiry if she did not find the people at Pompeii very uncongenial to her.

"Yes," she answered, quite simply, "I was very disappointed. The people are merely a crowd of fashionable idlers; there are no really intellectual people there at all. They talk about nothing but society, politics, and sport—all three topics that I loathe."

"My dear, we must try and take an interest in the life around us," put in Mr Leo. He felt, as a man of the world, that his wife was a little wanting in *finesse*.

"Well, you couldn't have expected to find all that is most illustrious in literature and art on this yacht, for instance?" said Mawnan, still smiling.

"That would have been quite the last thing I should have expected to find," answered Mrs Leo, in her most composed and superior voice.

"All that is most illustrious in literature and art! Oh, I hope I haven't fallen *quite* so low as that," said Mawnan, bursting out laughing.

But Mrs Leo said nothing. She had long discovered that silence is the golden road for scorn.

The rest of the party had listened to the conversation with varying degrees of amusement. Claud, who had in his heart long alternated between thinking Mrs Leo insufferably perfect and perfectly insufferable, was secretly delighted when any one ventured to offer chaff at the shrine of that divinity. Claudia, on the other hand, admired Mrs Leo's scorn of all the pettiness and littleness around her, and she felt inclined to take her part. Mrs Denbigh simply regarded the Leos as harmlessly eccentric literary or artistic people; and she spent her time in wondering how they came to Pompeii, and why they had been asked on to the yacht. She only wished that Mrs Leo would not so entirely monopolise the conversation, and that if she so disliked " merely fashionable idlers "—a dislike that was heartily reciprocated—she would keep away from them.

After lunch every one wandered up on deck. Mawnan got a deliciously comfortable deck-chair for Mrs Denbigh, and then seated himself beside

her. He smoked, and laughed, and chatted on in
the most entertaining way. He told her that he
had known Mrs Leo for many years—ever since
she was a tall solemn-eyed girl, and he had been a
youth coaching with her father, when he had an
idea of going into the army. "We used to go it
cat and dog—just as we do now; and yet I
really believe we respect one another at bottom.
I know I used to be in love with her. I believe I
once offered to her—yes, I know I did; because
she said, 'Lord Mawnan, I would rather be a
butcher's wife than be a soldier's,'—rather rough
on me, wasn't it? So I said, 'A butcher! I bet
you a fiver you marry some one worse than that.'
But, do you know, I've never ventured to remind
her of the bet since. It would be so confoundedly
awkward to decide who had won it."

Claudia wandered to the forecastle. She found
a chair for herself and a book, but she did not read
much. She was wondering why Mrs Leo, with her
high ideal and her intellectual aim, was after all so
repellent. "Is it," she said to herself, "simply because she has no manners; or is it not, after all,
something that goes deeper than that—a want of

genuine sympathy for all, even for the poor fashionable idlers around her ? "

Claud had been hovering near, restrained for a moment by a strange feeling of bashful uncertainty. He now came forward, and took another chair that was standing near her.

Claudia looked up and smiled. "I was wondering," she said, "whether one cannot live a good and noble life without making people dislike one, on account of what they fancy are one's airs of superiority."

"Of course," answered Claud, warmly. "I hold that the best-loved people are the really best, through all the history of the world. If you are thinking of Mrs Leo, it is not her superiority we dislike—though I fancy a good deal of that is not quite genuine—it is her want of tact and manners ; and then she is absolutely devoid of either sympathy or humour."

"You must not abuse her to me, for I am a great admirer of hers. I regard her with a vague awe, as though she were a visitant from another world. It is the very absence of sympathy and humour, and all the little everyday attributes of humanity,

that makes her like some majestic heroine in an
ancient tragedy. She isn't accidental, she is antique. I never understood, before I saw her, how
Helen of Troy could have existed; but now I can
fancy her led on, smiling, from one husband to another, still acquiescing in the purpose of the gods."

Claud moved a little nearer. "Don't you think,"
he said, "that people who have a high ideal, and
make a great profession of goodness, should try to
be more charming, more loved, than they otherwise
would be; and not try less, as so many good people
seem to do? For if they are repellent, they act as
a warning instead of an example."

"How true that is!" Claudia answered, softly.
"Good people seem so often to mean by their manner, 'I may be good, but I am not nice.'"

And so they chatted on. We need not follow
their casual talk any longer. The conversation of
two young people, when one of them is in love with
the other, is much the same as other young people's
talk. If there is any difference, it is that the lover's
words are generally slower in coming, and present
themselves in more disjointed sentences than usual.
It was delightfully warm; floods of sunshine filled

the air, and danced back in reflected brightness
from the tips of the waves. The two formed a
pretty picture as they sat there together: Claudia,
lying back in her chair, sheltered by a red parasol
from the glare of the deck and the glitter of the
sea; Claud leaning a little forward and talking
eagerly, his vivid face dyed with a brighter flush
by the same sunshine that lit up her smile and
turned her hair to gold. And behind them, as a
far-away background, was the endless, the match-
less blue of blending sky and billow.

CHAPTER VII.

THE morning bathe was a great institution at Pompeii. The beautiful marble swimming-bath was
generally crowded with men from ten to twelve,
who, after they had taken their dip, often lounged
about talking, and even stayed to breakfast, beneath the striped awning which sheltered the
little *caffè* at one end of it. The other end opened
directly on to the sea; and the spreading view
it gave was only broken here and there by a slim
bronze statue that glowed with a burning green or
brownish lustre in the hot air, and rested at the
marble rim, to be reflected, Narcissus-like, in the
ruffled waters at its feet. The classical air of the
whole scene was certainly not assisted by a scarlet
silk bathing-dress, edged with Roman lace, in which
Tottie daily disported himself, jumping up and down

in the shallow water at one end of the bath (he could
not swim), and generally singing little snatches of
comic song as he did so. But while he amused
himself thus, other people went on with their bathe
as though he were not in existence. Claud and
Darlington, for instance, were now sitting on the
edge of the bath drying themselves in the sunshine; sparkling drops trickled down them, and
dripped off their dangling legs into the water
below. Claud was smoking a cigarette, and half
lying back against one of the dark bronze statues.
Darlington, also smoking, found himself being lulled,
by the warmth and the gentle reaction after the cool
of the water, into the pathways that lead to sleep.
Claud stretched out his arm and recalled him from
this delicious loiter by touching him on the shoulder.

"I have something to tell you," he said, in ex-
planation. "The truth is, old boy—don't laugh at
me—but I'm really in love at last!"

"In love!" said Darlington, raising his eyebrows.

"Yes. Who do you think it is with?"

"Not the American girl, I hope," replied Darlington, quickly; "for I really believe I'm in love with
her myself."

"No—with Miss Denbigh." And then Claud
went on to explain how hopeless his love was.
He mentioned his own position—his strained re-
lationship with his uncle; and he asked Darlington to picture to himself Mrs Denbigh's maternal
horror when such a detrimental candidate presented himself.

Darlington, who was sanguine both from experience and disposition, assured him that relations
could always be got over. "And at the worst,"
he added, lightly, "you know, she may not really
care for you although you *are* in love with her.
But it's quite time we dressed." And dress they
accordingly did.

As they were strolling down the Forum they met
Lady Marlowe. She told Claud that Mr Cade was
in one of the billiard-rooms, and asked if he would
be kind enough to find him for her. She added that
Courier had arrived, and therefore she was anxious
that Mr Cade should join them at lunch. "Tell
him I am having lunch in my own rooms to-day;
and if you care to join us, I shall be delighted."

Darlington, in the meantime, had been pounced
upon and carried off by Mr Smythe, so that Claud

had to make his search alone. He soon, however, found Mr Cade in close confabulation with Mr Giles, and gave him Lady Marlowe's message. "That will do now, Giles; the Lords are to be tolerated for the present," said Mr Cade, in his loud, strident voice—a voice among whose tones the ominous idea of "Yield, or you are doomed," always seemed to lurk. Then he suggested to Claud that they should walk up to Lady Marlowe's together.

Mr Cade was a large, thick-set man, whose bull-dog neck and slightly sinister expression denoted determination and hinted at possible mischief. If he was not satisfied with the world (as it was at present), he was obviously satisfied with himself, which was much more important. He had begun life, as has before been mentioned, with the pro-fession of a temperance lecturer. But finding it more philanthropic than lucrative, he soon aban-doned it—for his love of his fellow-creatures was not so exceptionally keen as one might have judged from the tone of his speeches—and entered the tail-oring business, with large shops in the City and West End. Indeed, so successful was he both in

pushing his trade and in forcing his employees to
work for still longer hours and for still smaller
wages than the rival houses gave, that at last he
succeeded in ruining most of these, and finally
almost monopolised the wholesale tailoring business. And this will not be wondered at when the
reader is assured that the young gentlemen in the
city offices thought his "eleven and ninepenny
pants" were equal to the thirteen and sixpenny
pairs of other firms. Finding that his half-starved
workmen could only afford to live crowded together
like animals rather than men, he was naturally
anxious that they should be better housed (at some-
body else's expense). The first thing to be done
was to engraft upon the Liberal party a series of
Jacobin clubs (somewhat after the pattern of those
established during the French Revolution), and then
to delude the party with the impression that they
were merely an improved form of organised representation. But when once established, he quietly
proved to them that he had matured his machinery
in order to organise representation out of existence.
Members were turned into delegates; and, goaded
on by a hinted reign of terror they began to ac-

quiesce in his plans of plunder, his plots for robbery. He showed them how, by the fortunate conditions inherent in a democratic form of government, they could rob (from the very nature of the case) with absolute impunity; that whatever they might do, they would be perfectly safe. For could they not escape from Justice by wrapping the sacred ægis of the State around them, while at the same moment they were strangling Liberty among its folds ?

Mr Cade was, however, quite clever enough to have a social side, and it was this side which was presented to the company during lunch. He was a well-informed man, and the general conversation touched on the various topics of the day, steering clear of politics, as though to avoid "the shop." M. Courier chatted on about all that was newest in Paris. The fresh piece at the Palais Royal, "Le Bâton," was discussed. It was so successful, they were told, that Paris rang with a new song which had been made out of it—

"J'ai un bâton, un petit bâton."

Then the conversation passed over to London. Lady Marlowe explained to M. Courier that the struggle for existence had at last even invaded

Society; that the smartest young men in town had taken to the Stock Exchange, had taken to the stage. And she poured into his astonished ear the fact that one of her friends—a charming boy—had just joined the music-hall profession, and had already appeared at the Pavilion with immense success. All M. Courier could do was to murmur "Vraiment!" with an air of incredulous politeness.

"And the delightful thing is," went on Lady Marlowe, "that none of these young men in the least forfeit their social position, if they have once been taken up by Society. For if you are once in Society, you are privileged to do almost exactly what you like."

"Strange people, you English," murmured M. Courier. "Your country is supposed to be aristocratic, but with us such a thing would be impossible."

"Oh," put in Cade, "all Society wants is excitement. In England nothing stops them, if one or two of the right people set the example. It's a sign that the whole thing is at its last gasp, and will very soon come to an end entirely."

"Oh, please don't destroy us quite yet!" re-

sponded Lady Marlowe. "It is very pleasant at
present; and I know you really enjoy it yourself"
(which was quite true). "Although this is only
lunch, I am going to leave you, gentlemen," she
added, rising; "and then you can conspire in peace
together."

She passed out of the room. The two politicians
drew their chairs together, leaving Claud at the
table slowly demolishing strawberries.

At first the conversation, although it had taken
a political tone, confined itself more or less to
generalities. Mr Cade described the machinery
of the Caucus, and M. Courier regretted that
they could not manage something of the sort in
France.

"You Radicals," he went on, in his broken accent,
"can advance in England so much faster than we
can in France. For why? You have still the
aristocracy and the great landlords to hold up for
attack. We have no ruling aristocracy, and the land
is held by so many that we should have no chance
with that. Our great enemy is the middle class—
the *bourgeoisie*. But they are so numerous, so stupid,
so conservative, that they prevent everything." M.

Courier threw up his hands and eyebrows at this unaccountable effort of self-preservation.

"We have the same trouble, to a certain extent. All our small shopkeepers and that class are ratting —turning Conservative, you know. Why, I can't think; for their pockets won't be touched. At least," said Mr Cade, with his most magnanimous air, "I for my part have always intended that they shall be left alone."

"Ah, you happy man! you are in the Cabinet, you can control. I am a power, but somehow I am unaccountably omitted from every Government that is formed."

"Yes; your Governments are, after all, very reactionary. You see, we are blessed in England with an unwritten constitution; and so we can stretch it, and stretch it, to fit anything that we want, until——"

"Until it breaks up and has ceased to exist," put in M. Courier, with a laugh. "Yet somehow, out of your country, all over the world, your Conservatives are better liked."

"That is because of their flashy, unscrupulous, aggressive foreign policy," said Cade, with a little more warmth than he had yet shown—"that absurd sentiment which they cultivate, and call patriotism. Some of them want imperial federation with the colonies. As though we were likely to stand that! Now our plan is to lessen in every way the country's responsibilities—to try and avoid having any foreign policy, and to attend to our own affairs at home. We want slowly to dismember the empire (the very word 'empire' makes me sick), if it can be done without friction. And I assure you we are getting on. Ireland, I think, we can leave safely in the Prime 'Minister's hands; for I have no doubt, in a year or two, he will have contrived her arrival at such a pass that Englishmen will be only too anxious to grant her 'Home Rule.' The detachment of the Colonies, I think, may be also safely left to our present Colonial Minister. But the difficulty to me is India. I cannot see how we are to get rid of it, unless Russia is kind enough to take it."

Mr Cade, in his earnestness for the reconstruction of the empire, had entirely forgotten Claud's presence, and so he continued, "My private plan is to give her autonomy. You know what I mean,—

make her independent, and set up a representative
Government there—in the same way that we are
going to give Ireland a representative Government.
The Liberal party, led on by those d—— aristocratic Whigs, have crushed down and trampled on
the people of Ireland and India quite long enough.
And look what a saving of expense it will be!
I have drafted a bill for the purpose. I shall
show it to the Cabinet when I get back; but I
don't somehow fancy they'll like it. If they don't,
we must turn on the screw," concluded Cade, with
a wink.

"How conscientious you are!" cried M. Courier.
"You cannot bear to see any one oppressed—even
when you do it yourself."

"The Radical party are the conscientious party,"
replied Mr Cade, with dignity.

"And when you have got rid of all your responsibilities?"

"Then we shall be a happy little island to ourselves, with no foreign complications or entangle-
ments, no army and a very small fleet, with certainly no rich people, and I hope no poor ones.
Every man will have his two or three acres, his

pig or perhaps his cow. There will not be any unwholesome amount of liberty, and the people will be relieved from the government of the country by the machinery which I am setting up. The minority are no longer to trample on the majority, but the majority are to be absolutely autocratic. If that isn't Democracy, I don't know what is."

" A paradise, a paradise !" cried M. Courier. " Oh that I could only look forward to such a future for my poor France !"

" And I forgot to add—which is the most important thing after all—that we shall be sufficiently patriotic somehow to manage that we are always in office and power, and the other party always in Opposition."

" Ah, you are a real statesman !" put in M. Courier, not satirically, but quite innocently.

Claud looked up, his eyes flashing. He felt as though he had been participating in a treasonable plot, assisting in some unholy incantation wrought by a dark conspirator. " We think that Mr Cade is the greatest of his kind," he said. Then there was a momentary pause before

he added, " But we cannot hope that he will be
the last."

Mr Cade sprang round as though he had been
struck. He had forgotten Claud's presence for the
moment; and now that he was reminded of it, he
seemed inclined to express himself somewhat strongly for a statesman. Perhaps this idea occurred to
him, for he instantly restrained himself, and said,
with an awkward laugh, " I really forgot you were
there, Mr Brownlow. But I am not sorry that one
of your order should have heard what a plain-
spoken leader of your party thinks, who knows his
own mind and isn't afraid of calling a spade a
spade. When I talk about your party, I presume
you call yourself a Liberal and really are an aristocratic Whig."

" No; I am a Conservative."

" Your uncle calls himself a Liberal."

" He *is* one." Claud's temper was rising at the
underlying insolence in the man's tone and manner; but Mr Cade, on the contrary, had so far re-
covered his, as to tender a little (statesmanlike)
counsel.

" Come," he said, " let me give you one piece of

advice. You had better join us. We are the winning party, yours is the losing. It is always better to be on the winning side."

" No, thank you, I shall not change. I would rather do what I thought was right, even if it deprived me of the pleasure of helping you in your schemes of plunder, than be on the winning side in my country's ruin. Besides, I am not so sure that we may not succeed after all."

" Succeed, succeed!" said Mr Cade, testily. "Why, what the deuce can you succeed in?"

Claud, as he rose from the table, flamed up. "Succeed!" he said, and he looked like an angry young prince as he did so. "We may yet succeed in saving our country—from you." And he strode out of the room.

Out of the room he strode, and on until he reached the sea-shore. He sat down among the pebbles on the beach, still tingling with indignation. He himself was not sure why he felt so angry. Was it, he asked himself, merely a burst of temper at Cade's insufferable tone, or could it really be the indignation of his outraged patriotism? He laughed a little at the phrase—at the

idea of his patriotism being of a quality to be
"outraged." He hated all forms of posing. He
disliked people who professed to have such exquisitely sensitive natures that they could not help
feeling much more keenly than the rest of the
world about affairs which in no way concerned
them particularly. Why should he be more indignant at Cade's theories, he said to himself, than
any one else was? He was not constituted a
guardian of his country's honour and greatness.
And if he were, he would probably be unable to
save her from Mr Cade and his schemes.

"A democratic form of government is inevitable,
it seems. Indeed, have we not got it now? It is true
that no form of government could be more fatal to
the supremacy, or even existence, of such an empire
as ours. But that will not check its advent; with
some," thought Claud, with a bitter smile, "it will
be an additional incentive to force it upon us."
And then he recalled all the numberless sons of
England who would cheerfully die to save their
dear country from ruin, if only they saw the
way — men, even now, who were fighting her
battles and steering her navies, aiding her suffer-

ing ones, guiding her sinful ones, raising her lost
ones.

Yet they were scattered, outnumbered, outwitted.
Some were blinded by faction, and some were re-
pressed by their party ties, and all were helpless—
a hopelessly small minority. "For are we not
ruled entirely by numbers now?"

Claud really loved his country; and the specious
pretexts by which her poor people were slowly but
surely being enticed to accomplish her doom and
their own, seemed to his generous soul an unscrupulous sign of the criminal plots they concealed.
If the reader now thinks him a very foolish young
man, I can only point to his youth as a plea
for forgiveness; for one of the chief of youth's
numerous follies, we find, is intolerant hatred of
meanness, self-seeking, and treachery — a folly
which, while we deplore it, we are thankful to
know will be one of the first to be extinguished
by the growth of prudence and worldly experience.

And if the reader thinks that Claud had better
attend to his own business, instead of troubling
himself about patriotic affairs which in no way
concerned him, I can also hasten to comfort him

on this point also, by the assurance that Claud
was at this very moment engaged in some really
practical and important business of his own. A
dress which he had ordered for a grand fancy ball
that was going to be held the same evening had
just arrived, and he was now trying it on to see if
it fitted.

CHAPTER VIII.

THE ball was to be the most exquisite thing of its kind ever given on the Riviera. A large part of the Forum had been boarded over for the floor; and above, a vast awning had been stretched by cords in the approved classical manner. At the end farthest from the sea rose a glorious bank of flowers; but the sea end of the extemporised ball-room was left free to secure a refreshing view of the darkening sky and the quiet waters as they passed away to the drowsy outskirts of the approaching night.

As the evening drew on, servants might have been seen flitting here and there in their airy and delicate classical dresses. Lights woke up one by one; and each little spark lightly powdered the marbles around it with brightness. Glimpses of

fruit and of flowers heaped on tables laid out in
the temples, might have been caught by inquisitive eyes.   And then specials arrived from the
other towns on the coast, even coming as far as
from Cannes.   Mr Smythe was for once in the
highest of spirits.   Already dressed as the great
Mogul, he hastened here and ran hither.   He
smoothed the way for this person (probably a
grand-duchess), and he skilfully avoided the way
of that one (who was probably nothing more than
an old and valueless friend).

Gradually the marble Forum filled with people,
then suddenly flashed into dazzling brilliance as
the electric light burst on the night from its
thousands of opalesque lamps.   There was a sudden
revelation of high-bred princesses and lightsome
fairies ; noble lords and beautiful pages ; pretty
flower-girls and peasants; fisher-boys, matadors,
soldiers, and sailors : costumes of every age, and
from every country, clashing in a delicious confusion
of movement and colour.   The very air seemed to
palpitate — charged with the dreamy music, the
tinted lights, the delicate perfumes, and the reson-
ant murmur of hundreds of happy voices.   The

whole was immersed in a subtle glamour, alluring the senses, and leading them captive, as though seen with unearthly charm in some ancient magician's mirror.

Claud was there, dressed as a Florentine youth of the *cinque cento*. With his long striped tights, his short fanciful doublet all covered with puffs and slashes, and his little red cap with its single feather, which nestled so knowingly among his curls, he looked as though he might have slipped out of some old painting by Signorelli, or been a boon companion to one of those gentlest of warriors who fit on their dainty armour so gracefully in the frescoed "arts of war" at South Kensington. He called himself Tito; for since the events of the afternoon, he quite felt as though he had been conspiring against the liberties of his country. He was now leaning against a pillar, in order to watch the various groups passing backwards and forwards. Mrs Leo swept by, looking really most beautiful as the Duchess of Malfi. She did not dance; but she stood in her queen-like pre-eminence, crushing by contrast, she knew, the surrounding throng of mere butterflies—soulless, idealess

slaves of fashion. Then he thrilled for a moment
as he caught a glimpse in the distance of Mrs Denbigh and Claudia—Claudia looking, to him, more
lovely than ever, but dressed this evening in the
simple grey of a Sister of Charity. They passed out
of sight, and before he had time to move towards
them, Miss van Knut walked up to him. She was
dressed in a Japanese costume—that is, as a French-
ified, fancified, idealised Japanese Folly, such as
one might fancy M. van Beers could design. Tiny
masks hung by silver chains to her waist, their
eyes twinkling with unholy mockery. As she
walked, there were glimpses of impish mouths that
grinned out from the folds of her skirt. A quaint
little Japanese devil sat up on her hair, happily
posing himself with an air of serenity so diabolic
that one could not help laughing.

"What do you think of my dress?" she said in
a moment. "It was designed for me by a friend of
mine—a young artist—in Paris."

"It is so wonderful," said Claud, "that it has the
disadvantage of even taking some of one's attention
from the wearer."

"My! that's very pretty! I haven't heard any-

thing so pretty since I came to Europe. A young
girl feels the change when she comes to Europe,
I can tell you."

" The change ! "

" Oh yes; we are much more appreciated in New
York, you bet. There we are at a premium; here
poor women seem to be a drug in the market. And
it's the young men who are at a premium, and have
to be petted and coaxed and made much of—I'm
sure I don't know why."

" Because a really complete and charming young
man is such a wonderfully perfect production of
nature and training. To possess a son nowadays
is to possess a great but expensive luxury. It's
almost like having a steam-yacht. You shouldn't
have these luxuries if you can't afford them. But
what so many parents fail to grasp is that, if you
do indulge in these things, you *must* keep them up
properly."

" Men in Europe seem to think themselves very
precious and indispensable, I'm sure. Now in
America we don't 'keep up' young men; *they*
have to work for their bread, in order to keep up
the ladies and give them a lovely time. Do you

know anything about America? do you ever read any of our books?"

"Oh yes; a great many."

"Who is your favourite novelist?"

"I think Henry James. Many of his short stories are simply exquisite. He is so wonderfully subtle."

"Yes; we're told that the way in which a lady lifts her arm from a table in carrying a teacup to her lips may contain all the elements of a modern tragedy—which certainly shows subtlety, if not sense. We don't like him much in America. We don't think he does us justice."

"Not do you justice, my dear Miss van Knut!" cried Claud. "Why, he describes the most delightful Americans."

"We think his nice Americans are too English, and his nasty Americans are too—too——"

"American?" suggested Claud.

"Your manners are worse than mine," replied the young lady, and the masks round her waist gave a jangle of assent. "You've not only insulted my nation, but, what is worse, you've neglected me, and haven't asked me to dance yet."

"You must forgive me, and ask me to dance instead. As for American novelists and their characters, I think, do you know, in their heart of hearts the Americans are still a little envious of our upper classes."

"Oh, you think so, do you? We can get on very well without them, I'm sure." Then she changed her tone and continued, "Now we will dance, and I will tell you a secret." She dropped her voice, and half playfully whispered, "*They are*——"

Mrs Denbigh, like a *grande dame* of the last century, in her rich brocaded dress and her powdered hair, was watching the gorgeous scene— Claudia had left her to dance—and spending the time in conversation with people around. She had a very quick eye, and for some time it had been "on" Miss van Knut. She turned to her neighbour and said, "What an extraordinary nation the Americans are!"

"They are," said her neighbour.

"They are so irrepressible. An English girl in a horrible dress like that, who behaved in that simply disgusting way, wouldn't be tolerated for a moment. She flirts," said Mrs Denbigh, "as though she were a kitchen-maid. She hasn't even the decency to conceal her flirtations. And yet she's received, and seems actually popular."

"They say that a woman, to be popular nowadays, must be prepared to say *almost* anything herself, and to permit *quite* anything to be said to her," rejoined the other lady.

"Yes; but that is the extraordinary thing about those American girls. With all their impropriety of manner, they are really extremely particular about that sort of thing. But that makes it all the more dangerous. We must try and protect our young men from their snares." Mrs Denbigh was really rather relieved to see that the dangerous siren— as she thought her—had commenced to spin her charms round Claud; for Darlington was the one particular young man she was determined to shelter, "whatever the cost to herself," as she would have said.

"Perhaps, after all, it is only simplicity," said the other lady.

"I call it barbarity," Mrs Denbigh remarked, with a certain weight in her tone which was calculated to carry conviction. "The other day I

asked her what she thought of Lord Darlington—
I wanted to sound her, you know, and delicately
show her that people were noticing her conduct to
him—and she answered me with an exquisite calm-
ness of audacity, which I'm bound to say even a
duchess couldn't surpass: 'Lord Darlington—why,
I think he's just simply lovely, he's perfectly
sweet.' She called the eldest son of a peer
perfectly sweet—to me, a comparative stranger!
Why, you know, it's unheard of; it's almost beyond
the pale of civilisation."

While Mrs Denbigh continued to express herself
on the deformation of character produced by a new
country, and the awfully demoralising effect that
that character had on those of the Old World
it happened to cross (a kind of inverted strong-
drink-and-gunpowder theory), Darlington, in the
garb of a jockey, was having a "fine time of it."
He danced with one young lady and another,
flirting with each, in his naïve boyish way, as
desperately as the time allowed. And this, we
know, is painfully short (even when you are the
eldest son of a peer, and therefore assisted by
every properly brought up young lady with all

her might), if you have determined to dance
every dance throughout the evening.

He was searching about for one of his partners,
when he espied Miss van Knut. He rushed up to
her; and—dazed, let us hope, by the spell of the
dress on the sorceress—threw over his fair one,
and told Miss van Knut he was waiting for her
to dance with him.

She promptly surpassed him in unscrupulousness, and threw over an old German baron that
Mr Smythe had planted on her.

Round they floated to the magic of a Waldteufel
valse, played by the Monte Carlo band, which had
been brought over for the occasion.

"Now," said Darlington, when the music ceased,
"I will take you out for a little row on the
sea."

"Is it very naughty?"

Darlington assured Miss van Knut that every
one was doing it. And she thought she would not
go. At last, after much persuasion, he got her into
the boat, and pulled her out a little way from the
land. The waning moon had just risen. It still
had that unearthly luminous redness with which it

sometimes glows after rising, not giving light, but hanging in the sky as though big with mysterious portent. The sea was black and oily. And when they had pulled out some way, the lights of Pompeii made all around them seem darker by contrast.

"Stop, Lord Darlington ; I want to go back," said Miss van Knut from the darkness.

"I am going to pull you to Africa," replied Darlington, in a bantering tone.

And he had to be sternly commanded before the boat's head began to turn in a homeward direction.

"I suppose you don't have anything as gay as this in New York," suggested Darlington.

"I assure you we do; we've the very nicest society."

"The President, and all that sort of thing, of course."

"No, not the President, at least not generally. In America we are very select. And most of the Presidents are not received by the really high-toned families. I've been introduced to the present one, though."

"What was he like ? " inquired Darlington.

" I don't know ; I didn't see him. I was introduced through the telephone."

" Dear me ! Did you ring him up ? "

" Papa did. He rang him up to know if he could have the London legation ; and then he introduced me—after he had heard that he couldn't. But you mustn't think, from the people we know here, that we're not exclusive. Because in America we're very exclusive indeed. In Europe, you see, it don't matter."

" I suppose you won't know me when I come to New York," said Darlington.

" That depends on how you behave. But if you're good, I'll take you round myself and give you a really good time."

Thus the exquisite night passed on.

So charming was it to float seawards in a boat, so cool and delightful to wander about at the starlit end of the Forum, that the ball-room was thinned in its numbers, although there were plenty of happy couples left to dance the hours away.

And even the laughter and talk of the crowds thronging the snug little supper-rooms in the surrounding temples were mellowed and blended with streams of delicious music that flowed from the band.

Every one seemed happy. Miss Rattletubs, dressed as a female Doctor of Divinity, looked busy and pleased. She was not dancing this evening, she said—which was quite true, as she had not been asked; but she walked about, and made or renewed acquaintances here and there among the crowd. One of these renewed acquaintances was Mrs Denbigh. They had, strange to say, several opinions in common. One of them, a dislike of "that little American flirt," as they called her, was not touched upon at the present time; for poor Mr Smythe happened to pass at that moment, and Miss Rattletubs turned her attention on him.

"Look at that man," she said; "can't you see him in his young days serving behind the cheesemonger's counter, when he was simply called Smith. They say, you know, his real name is Smith."

Now in Society it was the fashion to tolerate Mr Smythe (on account of his philanthropic exertions in its behalf), but to laugh at him all the same. So Mrs Denbigh felt she might allow herself to smile, as she answered—

"Oh, come now! you know, I don't really believe in the shop. It's only a joke that some of the boys have invented. He's a good, useful creature, and is kept by Society, because he gets their things up for them. Besides, you know, we shouldn't be here to-night if it wasn't for him. He invented Pompeii."

At this moment Lord Mawnan came up and carried Mrs Denbigh off to supper. We need not describe the meal. It was like any other luxurious feast of the kind. But Mawnan, having taken Mrs Denbigh back to her seat, returned, as men will, to leisurely finish his own supper, unhampered by female attractions. He found Claud seated on one side of him, and at once broke into conversation, in his hearty enjoyable way.

"I've been dancing to-night," he said, "with the most delightful Japanese girl—at least she's really an American girl, don't you know. She makes all the ladies quite wild. She's really so awfully un-worldly and natural that, by Jove, they can't un-derstand such simplicity! She's quite like Gala-tea in the play, and they'll finish her off if they can. But she knows how to take care of herself, which Galatea didn't; and she's got a spice of

mischief in her when she's roused. She's awful
fun, too. What do you think she told me she's
been doing to-night? Why, she danced twice with
one of these Italian waiters. She pretended to
think he was an Italian prince in costume. But
she says that she found him much more amusing
than a real Italian prince, and much more polite
than an English one."

There was a good-looking young man in a uniform seated opposite to them. He had made one
or two remarks to Mawnan; and Claud inquired
who he was.

"He's called Redburn," answered Mawnan. "A
charming sort of fellow. He's rather a piquant
kind of mixture, too; for you wouldn't think he
was an artist, would you?"

"I thought he was in the army."

"That's a yeomanry uniform. He's a great riding
man—hunts, plays polo at Hurlingham, and so on.
Besides which, he paints little pictures in the most
advanced Franco-American style—Whistler—that
sort of thing; little things, all colour and tone,
that look equally beautiful whichever way you
turn them."

" He looks too close-cropped and well-groomed for an artist."

"Yes; he's not in the least artistic to look at, but I'm told his paintings are nothing else. I'll introduce you." And Mawnan proceeded to do so across the table. " Let me introduce the great coming R.A. and our future Lord Chancellor," he said, in his humorous, good-natured way.

" R.A. !" said Redburn, coming round to their side of the table. "Well, I never expected to be called an R.A.; but one never knows what one may come to some day." And then he and Claud fell to talking about Paris. He told him that the artist life there was really very pleasant, if you didn't mind roughing it and put all your English notions in your pocket. " Besides," he added, " I used occasionally to mitigate the Bohemianism of the life by disguising myself as a gentleman, and going to dine at the Café Anglais." Then, having finished their strawberries, they rose from the table; and Redburn went to look for M. Courier, whom he had slightly known in Paris, in order to introduce him to Mrs Denbigh, as that lady was anxious to make his acquaintance.

Claudia all this while had been dancing, and supping, and talking, doing all sorts of delightful things, with her heart full of happiness. For the one thing in society she really enjoyed was a thoroughly good dance. Now Darlington's turn had come. He walked up to her, and suggested that they should sit out their dance. "And then, you know, we can have a good talk about hunting," he said. "Don't you wish we were hunting now, instead of being stuck here with all these people?"

"Yes, yes; let us talk about hunting," she answered. And talk about hunting they did. They discussed the hounds and the hunters, the runs they had had in the winter, the adventures through which they had passed. For a talk about hunting need never end for lack of material, when two young and ardent riders combine to describe and enjoy its delights together.

There is the "meet" in the early spring morning, when the mist still lies lightly along the valleys. The whole neighbourhood seems to be gathering at the appointed place—often an open space in the midst of a village street. On one side, the old

grey church, and its slumbering yew-guarded
churchyard; and on the other, the sleepily digni-
fied inn that has known better days,—its quaint
little bar now awakened and bustling—its ancient
yard filled with grooms and their masters, with
mounting riders and unharnessed dog-carts.

The street is blocked with a happy crowd. There
are men in pink and in black, spotless and radiant
—their white breeches, with tiny bows tied at the
knee, shining above their polished "tops" and their
glittering spurs. There are young men in brown;
boys (home for the holidays) mounted on ponies;
sturdy young farmers on cobs; and ladies and
girls, glowing and flushed by excitement and exercise, dressed in short, dainty, tight-fitting habits,
and patting their horses' necks, while they talk to
their friends around; there are others in dog-carts,
who have driven over to "hunt upon wheels" if
they can—and if not, to see as much of the fun
as possible. On the pavements stand rows of
spectators. The villagers look on with stolid interest, the children cluster around with broad
smiles of intelligence.

Every man feels that all are his neighbours for

once—all his companions—with one common interest, one all-absorbing delight; until at last the master, the huntsmen, the whips, and the hounds come up. Then the chatter redoubles, girths are finally looked to, every one settles himself in his saddle, all the horses' heads turn in the same direction, and the field trot away together behind the hounds and the huntsmen.

We have neither the time nor the space to follow the day any further: to picture the scattered field, waiting down by the sheltering covert—the knowing ones planted in likely places, and both horses and men all alert with restrained expectation; to follow the glorious run — half a lifetime of happy emotions, supreme excitements, and hair-breadth escapes crowding into the flying minutes.

We cannot follow; but Darlington and Claudia did, in their talk. They rode their hunts over again; they took their hedges; they distanced competitors; they were in at the death. They were breathless—with mere description; and glad recollections alone filled their eyes with responsive sparkle.

"Have you ever noticed one difference between

horses and dogs?" Claudia went on, when Darlington had pulled up breathless. "A dog is aristocratic in his ideas. He is essentially a courtier.
He discriminates in a moment between the kitchen
with its inhabitants, and the master of the house
with his friends. A horse, on the other hand, is
democratic. He makes no distinctions; but he
(like many democrats) is fond of pageant, pomp,
and glitter."

"I never thought of that before," answered Darlington. And by way of saying something, he
remarked—"I suppose you've had a lot of dances
with Claud?"

"No. I have not seen him all evening."

"Not seen him!" burst out Darlington. "I should
have thought——" and he paused and blushed
with boyish awkwardness at his blunder. Then
with a change of tone he suddenly added, "But
here he comes at last." And Claud walked up to
them as he did so.

Claud's heart was beating. He had tortured
himself by postponing the moment for fear of
appearing too eager; for fear of Mrs Denbigh; for
the numerous reasons a young man assigns when

for once he is seized with a modest timidity. And now, though the ball was nearly over, he had come to claim one valse, and that valse was granted. As they stood up to begin, he asked Claudia if she had yet been out for a row; and when he found that she had not, proposed that, instead of dancing, they should have a short pull on the sea.

Claudia hesitated, for she doubted if Mrs Denbigh approved of dances being "sat out" in boats. Claud still pressed her, and so she yielded at last. "You ought," she said, "in that costume, to play a mandolin. Haven't you got one that you could bring with us?" Claud asked if a banjo would do as well; and being told that even that was better than nothing, he fetched his from his room, as they passed by on their way to the landing-stage.

As soon as they reached the boat, Claudia said that for once she was going to row, and Claud must sit in the stern and sing to her. He had to give in, after demurring a little, and the boat glided out to the night under the steady stroke of Claudia's sculls. Claud strummed in a gently vague way on

his banjo, until they had got out a little distance,
when he ventured to sing one or two nigger songs.
Claudia asked him for "Oh, dem Golden Slippers!"
and his voice gave the sorrowful air all its wistful sadness — an air vaguely suggesting the soft
crooning prayer of an alien race for the happier
days of long ago.

"Thank you," said Claudia slowly, and she
ceased for the present from rowing. "When shall
we have such a beautiful night again? Everything
is so still and so calm. We might be in some land
of other days."

"Yes," said Claud, and his fingers still hinted an
air on the murmuring banjo-strings :—

> "'The moon shines bright. In such a night as this,
> When the sweet wind did gently kiss the trees,
> And they did make no noise,—in such a night——'

You know the rest."

"'I would outnight you did nobody come,'"
answered Claudia, appropriately.

"But nobody does come."

"Yes, Mr Cade—I mean, he comes into our
conversation. I want to know why he is so
hated."

" On such a night why need we mention Cade ? "
asked Claud, with the look of a poet who is interrupted in the midst of a recitation of one of his own
works. " But if he must come," Claud continued,
" he shall find his match. He is hated, then,
partly because he is feared, and partly because he
is unprincipled."

" But he is very clever," said Claudia, in an
unsatisfied tone.

" His unscrupulousness is his cleverness, I think.
Or if you like to put it the other way, he is clever
enough to know that he can succeed best by being
unscrupulous."

" Well, I think people are very hard on him.
But then, you know, I am a great Radical."

" A Radical ? "

" Yes. For when one sees all the poverty and
all the misery around one, how can one help—how
can any one help—wishing and trying to improve
their lot ? I long that I could do something to help
them."

" I feel the same for the poor that you do. But,
do you know, that is exactly the reason why I'm
a Conservative. Must we still, for the thousandth

time, contradict the monstrous assertion that the poor and their welfare are less to us than to the Radicals? They mature them for tools. We wish to teach them the self-reliance of men. They would turn them into poor Socialists; we into patriotic Englishmen. But we can't talk any more politics at present. The night is too beautiful for anything but——" then he caught himself up, and said " poetry. As Shakespeare would say—

     " ' On such a night all politics must pall.'

And as for Cade—well, to show you the kind of man he is, I will tell you what I heard him say to Courier only this afternoon; only please don't tell any one else, as I heard it in confidence." And Claud repeated as much of their conversation as he could remember. When he had finished, Claudia proposed that they should return. She thought their dance must be over now. Claud thought, though he did not say so, that not only their dance, but the two following ones, must be also passed. He asked her to let him pull them back. They changed places; yet when Claud had possession of the sculls, they did not seem to move with any

undue briskness through the water. They rather
loitered caressingly, and scattered it back on itself
in bright drops of liquid fire.

"A drifting boat lulls one so gently ; it rocks all
one's nature to sleep, till it almost bears one away
from one's self."

"Yes, one floats on and on, and dreams one will
never wake," said Claud, in a tone of languid acquiescence.

"And, therefore, I don't wish to drift any longer,
please," put in Claudia, with a light in her eye.
"Try and pull us a little faster."

Claud dipped his sculls in again, but again took
up the drifting talk. "Think of poor Maggie, in
'The Mill on the Floss,' all that long warm day,
floating down to the sea, as passive as the victim
of an incantation—almost irresponsible and wholly
unresisting."

"Poor, poor Maggie. She, I think, is my favourite heroine. Sinned against, not sinning. The
victim of fate—of the hard, unrelenting, inexor-
able circumstances around her. And yet how she
struggled ! Are we all as powerless in the hands
of fate, do you think ?"

"Not powerless, if we determine to shape our fate for ourselves. Otherwise, if we let ourselves drift at the mercy of every circumstance, we may make a wreck of our own life—and others." He spoke softly, yet quickly. There seemed a swift rush of sweet thoughts through his brain, keeping time with his beating heart. He struggled against it, dreading it, only half comprehending it. "But floating here, as we are," he continued (for the blades of the sculls had by this time ceased to dip, and were now in motionless rest on the water)— "it is all so lovely, that Shelley alone can express what one feels :—

> "'My soul is an enchanted boat,
> Which like a sleeping swan doth float
> Upon the silver waves of thy sweet singing;
> And thine doth like an angel sit
> Beside the helm conducting it,
> Whilst all the winds with melody are singing.
> It seems to float ever, for ever,
> Upon the many-winding river,
> Between mountains, woods, abysses,
> A paradise of wildernesses !'"

He paused.

"Go on, please," said Claudia.

" ' Till, like one in slumber bound,
  Borne to the ocean, I float down, around,
  Into a sea profound, of ever-spreading sound.
  Meanwhile thy spirit lifts its pinions
  In music's most serene dominions—
  Catching the winds that fan that happy heaven.
  And we sail on, away, afar,
  Without a course, without a star,
  But by the instinct of sweet music driven,—
  Till through Elysian garden-islets
  By thee, most beautiful of pilots,
  Where never mortal pinnace glided,
  The boat of my desire is guided—
  Realms where the air we breathe is love,
  Which in the winds and on the waves doth move,
  Harmonising this earth with what we find above.' "

He ceased, and leant a little forward. Neither spoke. The stillness was strangely impressive, only broken now and again when little delicate bursts of music came fluttering out to sea on the wings of the wind. The moon, now pale and risen, was veiled by a film of silver cloud. The sea was dark, reflecting the overshadowing night, but the ripples were touched by a soft phosphorescent glitter. Claud suddenly realised that he was in the presence of one of the supreme moments of his life.

A calm irresistible force seemed to master him. It possessed itself of him; it impelled him to speak. And the words that he uttered flowed from him—not consciously formed by his mind, but in tones that were strange to his ear, so that he listened to them as though to a stranger speaking.

"I love you, Claudia; will you be mine?" he heard them say. And his eyes, preternaturally keen, saw her flush, and then turn very pale. His arms stretched out as though they would press her to his bosom. Then he heard her say, "Take me back—this is cruel of you;" and he saw her head bend over her hands, as she burst into tears.

"Forgive me," he cried. "I know I ought not to have spoken to you here—now."

She looked up, and with a supreme effort controlled her tears. "You had better speak to my mother," she said. "We will try and forget our mistakes."

"Forget—forget my mistake! Forgive it, for I could not help it; but do not forget it. Now you know that I love you—shall always love you. I

will speak to your mother. Till then, let us be as
though nothing had happened."

"I am the victim of fate," she said, trying to
smile. "I can't struggle; I am too weak, I think."

And, until they reached the shore, not another
word was spoken.

CHAPTER IX.

THE whole of Pompeii had naturally gathered in the Forum for the ball. All the servants even had gone, either to help or to see as much of the fun as they could.

And therefore the outlying streets lay deserted and silent. The very breeze, which so wooingly tended the brightly lit festival and the calm sea beyond, seemed here to have turned somewhat chilly. Only the thin waning moon looked down with the same calm insistence. And by the pallid light she gave, the black shadowed silent streets might have been those of that other city she also looked down on, now standing lifeless and deserted beneath the awful shade of its lurid destroyer: a ghostly corpse, reconquered from the tomb.

Yet in one of the smaller rooms near the entrance

a light was burning. And if a wandering couple or an inquisitive passer-by had been injudicious enough to intrude, they would have found Mr Giles (who scorned balls, and indeed was unnecessary to their success) entertaining an unpleasant-looking individual with cold brandy-and-water.

We will take a sample of their conversation in order to show the reader its drift, and then pass on to pleasanter people and subjects. (And we must again remind him that this is not a history, but a romance—a romance of to-morrow—with a very different sort of Government ruling to any one we may have at the present day.)

"We don't want any more outrages—indeed we really can't do with any more, just at present," Mr Giles was saying, with a certain incisive earnestness. "The English people have short memories, and are easily fooled. If you will only stop them now, the Prime Minister will get you Home Rule. He wants it himself, and only the doubts of his Cabinet hold him back."

"The money from America is the troublesome thing," said the unpleasant-looking man. "The Americans, you see, naturally won't subscribe unless they are sure of their money's worth. Now a good outrage or murder, or even a dynamite explosion with nobody killed, pleases them wonderfully, and quickens up the flow of money tremendously; because then they see we are earning it fairly. A few weeks ago, for instance, when a lot of old women held another old woman down for dogs to bite and worry her legs, and that boycotted man had his ears and his cheeks sliced off with razors, the money began to come in tremendously fast, and kept up for several weeks afterwards. You know we must think of our livelihood, even before the claims of Home Rule."

"Oh, I know, I know," replied Giles, in a sympathising voice. "It's very hard on you, I allow. But can't you tell them in America you're saving up all your outrages till the Conservatives come in next time?—if they ever do. Then we can have a double supply. You'll get the money, and we shall get the advantage of their policy being a failure."

"I will try; I will do my best," said the unpleasant man. "You know we should starve if it wasn't for the subsidies." He seemed still hankering after the forbidden delights of outrage, for he continued, "If we could only now tie a landlord to a stake, and roast him slowly to death with green fagots in the midst of his native village. You've no idea what a lot of money that show would draw. Why, we should all make our fortunes, and be able to retire from business."

"Oh, you mustn't do that; pray, don't do that," cried Giles, in absolute alarm. "You've no idea how anything *definite* of that sort upsets the English people. You can't conceive what a row they'd make, or how very unreasonable they would be. It might put off Home Rule for twelve months at least. Besides which, you know, it really would be rather cruel, and the Prime Minister would be extremely annoyed—extremely annoyed; although, of course, he would understand that it was only a regrettable incident natural to the present unsatisfactory state of affairs. But even if he wished to overlook it, his colleagues wouldn't permit him to do so."

Then they fell to discussing details, which would not be of general interest, and so we will drop the curtain.

The next day arose (as each day eternally rises) alike on the evil and on the good. On Claudia, sleeping soundly after a restless night; and on Claud, waking anxiously, wondering how he should break the ice with Mrs Denbigh. He felt that the cold plunge would have to be taken without any mitigating preliminaries. And he doubted if she would extend him a helping hand. She might even retard his efforts by assisting to freeze him.

Can we not all imagine the horror of that first interview with the stern parent, even though we may never ourselves have experienced it? The pause at the door; the particular make of the carpet, which we examine so long and so earnestly; the haggard attempt at everyday conversation; the awful moment when the plunge is taken, and we feel ourselves mentally toppling down like a house of cards. Our eligibility, income, advantages, and expectations (recalled and reviewed for the occasion), now shrivel up with a horrid persistence, as we try to present each in turn in as favourable a light as possible. The parent is on the alert; all the parental instincts are aroused, and we are exposed to a pitiless scrutiny. The whole is simply a waking nightmare, and it is no wonder that poor Claud mentally fingered it with a certain amount of dread apprehension.

As he walked along the streets—he had only a few yards to go—he did not notice the passers-by, or even the sunshine. He noticed nothing, and only knew that he was thinking, "What a fool I am going to make of myself!"

Mrs Denbigh was at home, and received him kindly. He tried to talk of the ball, of the people who were there—of anything he could think of. And although she answered him with polite responsiveness, he felt she was wondering all the while what had brought him there so early. At last he said, in a voice that was strange to himself—

"I have come to ask you, Mrs Denbigh, for a great—a great sacrifice. I have come to ask you for your daughter."

He thought that the phrase was pedantic; he wondered if it was also ludicrous. He looked at her. She was quite calm; and he had expected her to be surprised—even shocked.

"Perhaps," he said to himself, "she is accustomed to receive such proposals;" and he could not help adding, "perhaps accustomed to refuse them also."

"I admit you have taken me by surprise, Mr Brownlow," she said in a sweet voice, but without any tone to indicate the taking. "You have only known one another for such a short time. I think that before anything further occurs—I mean before you say anything to Claudia—you ought to see a great deal more of each other. Besides which, before I can sanction your suit, there are many other things to be considered."

Claud blushed. He glanced up with a pleading look in his eyes—eyes which, at times, were as eloquent as a dumb animal's—and said, "You will forgive me, I know, but—but I forgot myself last night—for a moment; I told your daughter how much I loved her."

Mrs Denbigh rose abruptly.

"What did she answer?" she asked, with a firm quickness.

"Only, 'Ask my mother,' I think."

"She is a good girl," said Mrs Denbigh, in a tone of reassured authority. "And now, Mr Brownlow, under the circumstances, I must tell you that I consider you made a mistake; not only a mistake, but a dishonourable mistake as well."

"Dishonourable! Oh, Mrs Denbigh, not dishonourable."

His eyes almost filled with tears as he also rose.

"My love is so great that it overflowed, and now I have come to confess it all to you."

"If it is likely to overflow again, my daughter had better not run the risk of causing it by seeing you," said Mrs Denbigh, a little drily.

"But you don't—you won't tell me, I must not hope!" broke out Claud.

"You are very young. You have at present no means of supporting a wife. I speak to you quite frankly; it is the kindest way in the end."

"I will get my uncle to write to you about—about my income and prospects, and all that."

"I think that will be the best plan; but, at the same time, I must warn you that there are already others in the field."

"Already," murmured Claud. He had nothing else to say. He vaguely wondered who the others were, and if this was the way that their offers were received. But he tried to smile as he answered—

"Even yet I shall venture to hope, for she knows that I love her."

"If you speak to her in the future, it must be as a—as a slight acquaintance. It would be better to do so, than for it to appear as though we had quarrelled."

"It shall be as you wish."

"And I trust to your honour as a gentleman not to say a word more to my daughter on the subject of love till you have asked my consent."

"I promise," answered Claud. Then he looked up, and said, "Have you forgiven my indiscretion?"

"I forgive you," she said, holding out her hand (but she had not). And Claud walked out into the blinding sunlight, and on to the sea-shore, feeling as though he had been crushed and almost trampled on, and yet not being able to find where the injustice lay.

"It must be her manner," he said to himself. "Not her words, but her manner of saying them."

On the sea-shore he found Darlington. He told him all, and they wondered who the "others" could be. Neither of them remembered that prudent

mothers sometimes not only keep "others" con-
veniently on hand, but have been known even to go
so far as to manufacture "another" out of a youth-
ful great personage without either his knowledge
or consent.

Darlington, for instance, never for a moment
thought that when Mrs Denbigh talked about
"others being in the field," she meant that she
hoped and expected that he would be caught there.
He comforted Claud, and promised to do all that he
could for him with Mrs Denbigh. They were very
old friends; and Darlington said in his confident
way that he would use all his tact to talk Mrs
Denbigh over.

So the days passed on. There were lunches on
yachts, and picnics up among the vine-covered
hills, where donkeys were ridden, and wild flowers
picked, and oranges eaten fresh from their dark-
leaved trees. There were boating-parties and
driving-parties; excursions to Nice and to Monte
Carlo. Whatever else there might be, there was
always lawn-tennis going eternally every day, from
early morning till sunset. Miss van Knut was the
life of every party she joined; and she joined a

great many. She laughed and chattered (she was even known in strict private to mimic her mentors). She appeared in a great many lovely dresses, always shaded by a large parasol, and cooled by a great crimson fan. She was generally followed by Darlington, who turned up with a kind of unexpected irregular certainty. They were the best of friends, but she was more than a match for him. She chaffed him unmercifully; and if he had ever had any intention of being sentimental (which he hadn't), she would have crumpled him up and sent him home in an envelope, as she would herself have subsequently expressed it.

He had no intention of being sentimental. He was not in love; and the whole fun of the flirtation to him was its being conducted on the American principle, of no love being involved, or even implied.

As the young lady was an American young lady, of course no one could say anything; and Darlington took advantage of his privilege accordingly.

Miss van Knut, on her side, liked Darlington extremely, but it must be conceded that some of the warmth of her friendship with him was caused by her mischievous love of witnessing the obvious alarm of all the other ladies.

We have not as yet seen anything of her father. Mr van Knut was a thin shrewd man, with a kind, worn, clever face, a black beard, now turning a little grey, and a manner which was at once both determined and unassuming. He was of course, to a certain extent, apparently effaced by his daughter, seeming at times to be rather a courier than a companion, and rather a companion than a parent. But this subordination was, after all, superficial, for in every important matter, whenever he "put his foot down," his word was law. At Pompeii he chiefly amused himself by taking long walks, his head always shaded by a big white umbrella; and he was often accompanied by one of the other gentlemen of the place. He was extremely good company. He was well-informed, and his natural shrewdness, reinforced by a certain dry humour, gave to his conversation a delightfully American flavour. Besides which, he was supposed to be a great authority on American railroads. When he and his companion were far on in their walk, and their conversation had tended towards confidence, he was often cross-questioned upon the momentous subject of securities; the safety or danger of various "mortgage bonds" and "debenture bonds" was discussed; and not even the "ordinary stocks" were ignored, although often condemned.

Mr van Knut had struck up a great friendship with Mr Leo. The latter, although, above all things, transcendental and idealistic in his writings, was not without a certain practical common-sense in everyday affairs. Leaving entire artistic and literary consistency to his wife, he edited his Review, for instance, with decided success. He knew the worth of "names," as well as the value of ideas; of the desirability of advertisements, as well as the delight of spreading enlightened ideas among those who were willing to give sixpence a-week to receive them.

And even if his noblest and most disinterested views for the future improvement of mankind had spread with a conquering force through Society, he would still have been wholly dissatisfied had the balance between receipts and expenditure not been generously in his own favour. He therefore found Mr van Knut not only extremely useful as a kind of exhaustless well out of which he could pump ideas on America, but also a practical person who told him where he could place in safety the earnings from all his struggles on behalf of humanity.

Mr van Knut's admiration of Mr Leo was caused by that gentleman's liberal knowledge and wide attainments. Mr van Knut had a great admiration for culture. And it was tempered by the slightest suspicion that Mr Leo was just—just a little bit of a humbug. For Mr van Knut had a brutal contempt for a humbug. His feelings towards Mrs Leo, however, were simple and entirely unmixed. They began by regarding her as a dread divinity in the world of thought, and they ended by thinking her rather a foolish woman in the world of men.

Miss Rattletubs all this time was not only writing her " Letters to a Brother," with a view to subsequent publication, but was also contributing an occasional article to the ' Morning Gazette.' She frequented Mrs Denbigh's society, partly in order to be, as she expressed it, " in touch " with the fashionable world, and partly because Mrs Denbigh was " very nice " to her. For Mrs

Denbigh, with her accustomed acuteness, recog-
nised " a power" in Miss Rattletubs, and she
always propitiated "a power" when she found
one.

Claudia spent most of her time with her mother.
She knew instinctively that Claud had been discouraged. She also knew that she did not love
him—or rather, she thought that she did not, and
told herself so, when she ventured to think of
him ; for what maiden knows her own heart at the
moment it flutters before the first rush of hot love
from another's ? She dare not let her mind dwell
on the tender events of that lovely evening. She
only felt that the memory of them was filled with a
wistful sweetness. Claud haunted the secret chambers of her heart, and would not be put forth. And
if she, in truth, almost cherished him there, it was
wholly unconsciously, for she believed she expelled
him whenever his yearning face and his burning
words rose up in opposed recollection. She was a
little weary of all the gaiety. Pompeii was really
too gay. She was restless, and longed to return to
England ; so that when Mrs Denbigh told her one
day that they were invited to afternoon tea with

the Princess Chioggia, she accepted the news with
indifference, and even forgot to consider what dress
she should wear.

The Princess Chioggia was one of the handsomest
women in Europe. She was a Hungarian, who had
married a Roman prince; but her sphere of activity was not confined to the little round of scanty
duties, and scantier pleasures, which is usually
trodden so circumspectly by Italian ladies. For
not only was she one of the handsomest women in
Europe, but she also had one of the finest physiques
as well, with a carriage—a *manière*—more regal
than that of most royal princesses themselves.
Yet, although in Society she was, above all things,
a princess, she climbed mountains in Switzerland,
hunted in England, swam splendidly, rode exquisitely, and danced divinely.

Her beautiful rooms were now thronged with
people at afternoon tea. The inner room was built
in exact imitation of one of the courts at Pompeii.
In the centre, a marble basin of clear water, in
which gold-fish swam, reflected the sky above. The
marble floor was covered with Eastern rugs. The
red-tinted walls were sprinkled with rosy Cupids

and baby-loves archly playing amid a delightful jumble of grinning masks, delicate flowers, and antique arabesques.

Rich curtains hung over the doorways, at intervals pushed aside when some nineteenth-century worldling was ushered in by (what looked like) a beautiful young Greek slave, dressed in a cream-coloured tunic, and crowned with a wreath of white lilac.

There were already a crowd of people assembled before the curtain was once again pulled back and Darlington entered. When he had found the Princess, and said all that is usual on such an occasion, he wandered on until he settled down by Miss van Knut. She would not talk to him before he had fetched her an ice. At last he came back with two (having captured one for himself as well), and then she resigned herself to a long conversation.

" What fools those fellows look dressed up like that!" Darlington began. " Why can't they have the servants here dressed in a proper livery ? "

" That would spoil it all. I think they're just lovely. I'm afraid you've no soul for art."

" No, I don't think I have much."

"Neither have I, between ourselves—at least I'm not struck dumb with awe by Botticelli or Carpaccio."

"I don't know who they are."

"Ah! you see, I'm more cultured than you. But then I've travelled in Italy and improved my mind. I shocked Mrs Leo the other day, when she said that the angels in the round Botticelli at Florence were bending their heads in adoring unison, by saying that I was certain they'd just screwed them down on one side simply to get in the frame. And what do you think she said?" Miss van Knut went on, mimicking her manner in the most delightful way. "She said, '*You* would naturally expect angels to compress themselves into a frame.' So I replied, 'Oh no, I'm quite content when ladies do so.' You know what I mean," she said, looking at Darlington.

And Darlington did, for he burst out laughing.

Miss van Knut having touched on her point, glided off, and returned once more to the scene around them. "This may be art; but in spite of that, it's awfully pretty (why I dislike most art is, that it's so terribly ugly), and we might be dear old Romans again."

"That is what Claud is always saying—'the classical life revived,' and that sort of thing. But I don't want the classical life revived, and I should hate to be a dear old Roman."

"Mr Brownlow hasn't looked so cheerful the last day or two."

"Can you guess why?"

"Yes."

"I'm sure you can't."

"I can—because he is in love."

"How do you know?" cried Darlington in astonishment.

"Oh, I know, I know; *I* have got a pair of eyes. And I could tell you the lady too, if I wished to be indiscreet."

"I can't think why the mother discourages it," said Darlington.

"I can. She has another young gentleman in view."

"Who?"

"That would be telling still more than I ought. The other day the young lady's mother asked me what I thought of a certain young man. I told her that I thought him just simply—well, I won't say what I said. She asked me to excuse her speaking plainly to me ; but as I had no mother, and wasn't a European (I am sure she thinks I am really a savage, and tattooed underneath my clothes), she was sure—and so on, and so on. I ought to know that it wasn't usual in England for young ladies to call the sons of peers simply sweet: besides, in this instance the young man was not —was not quite free."

" You don't mean to say she had the impertinence to talk about me like that. What does she mean by saying I'm not free ? " cried Darlington, angrily.

" So I replied," continued Miss van Knut, not taking any notice of the interruption, " ' You are quite right, Mrs Denbigh. And next time he's free, I'll let you know.' "

" But what can she mean about me ? " persisted Darlington.

" She thinks you are in love with her daughter, and therefore she has discouraged Claud. Now I want you to be very serious for once, and talk business with me, Lord Darlington," Miss van Knut continued, with a confidential air. " We must appear as though—well, as though we were nearly

engaged, and then she will give you up and encourage Claud."

" Oh, what fun !" cried Darlington.

" But mind it is only acting—only pretence. I
put you, sir, on your honour, never to take advantage of my generosity—I mean of my ingenuity."

" What a capital joke! What a score off Mrs
Denbigh! And I can't help laughing when I think
of my mother's face."

" Your mother !"

" Yes; she reckons to superintend all my *amours*,
you know. She asks likely girls down to stay at
Fieldhurst—that's our place in the country—and
all that sort of thing."

" But your mother mustn't ever hear of this. It
is only for a few days, in order to conquer Mrs
Denbigh. See, she is sitting over there now." Miss
van Knut's eyes sparkled with fun. " Go over,"
she said, " and just hint it to her, and see how she
looks."

Darlington sprang up. Miss van Knut tried to
stop him, but it was too late. Besides a mischievous delight in shocking Mrs Denbigh, he
wished at the moment to pay her out for retain-

ing him, as it were. So he quietly walked up to her and said, in a *nonchalant* tone, "I have come, Mrs Denbigh, for your congratulations. I'm engaged to Miss van Knut."

Mrs Denbigh caught her breath for a moment; and then, in the sweetest voice and with the kindest smile, she said, "I wish you all happiness, Darlington. Take me to Miss van Knut, that I may congratulate her—on her success."

Darlington gravely led Mrs Denbigh across the room. But before they had come to where Miss van Knut had been sitting, she jumped up and came forward to meet them. She blushed a little, and said hurriedly, "I hope Lord Darlington hasn't been saying anything silly."

"Nothing silly," replied Mrs Denbigh, in a clear slow voice. "On the contrary, he has been telling me of your engagement, and I have come to congratulate you."

Miss van Knut turned on Darlington, and in a tone in which amusement struggled unsuccessfully with distress, she said, "Lord Darlington, I am very angry at your being so silly." Then turning to Mrs Denbigh, she went on—

"It is only one of his foolish jests. I am afraid he has been playing a sort of childish practical joke on both of us, Mrs Denbigh."

Mrs Denbigh was deeply shocked. She was filled with a general impression of the extreme impropriety, the more than suggested vulgarity, of the whole scene. She felt sure in her own mind that somehow it was all due to Miss van Knut. Probably that young lady had first played a practical joke on Darlington, by suggesting to him the suitability of his making himself her husband. So that it was with rising indignation she turned to Miss van Knut and said—

"Whether it is a theoretical or a practical joke, Miss van Knut, it is obviously one in which no young lady should—I may say could—participate. Although, Lord Darlington, you are too young to appreciate either the value or the worthlessness of young ladies, you can at least understand that your joke has placed us all in a very unpleasant situation."

Darlington, blushing and filled with confusion, looked from one to the other. He was not sure if Miss van Knut was really pained, or if she was simply controlling her sense of the ludicrous. He

knew that he wanted to get rid of Mrs Denbigh,
and he did not mend matters by telling her that if
she would only leave them, he would find out
whether he had been premature. Miss van Knut
had flamed up at Mrs Denbigh's words. She
thought that they skilfully covered an insult, and
her voice trembled slightly as she said—

"In America, Mrs Denbigh, it would be considered more considerate, kinder, even better bred,
for a lady to accept a scene like this in the spirit
in which it was offered—especially when the joke,
though a poor one, was at another lady's expense."

Mrs Denbigh turned round and retraced her
steps, with a firm determination to let Darlington's
mother, the Countess of Downstreamdown, know
everything with as little delay as possible. Indeed,
Miss van Knut was so charmingly original, so dar-
ingly unconventional, she wore such extraordinary
dresses with such a fascinating air, and was altogether so unusual—unusually charming, most of
the men said—that Mrs Denbigh was not the only
lady who regarded her with an air of extreme dis-
approval. They said to each other, "These American girls will do *anything*, and say *anything* also."

By which they meant that Miss van Knut was capable of saying anything—even something unpleasant—about themselves. And they always seemed to tacitly imply that she was really a savage, who might at any moment be expected to burst through the thin veneer that civilisation had covered her with, and appear in her native war-paint and feathers. The Duchess of Man, for instance—herself a lady who, if she had been simply Mrs So-and-so, would have probably been refused admission to any respectable household—remarked to Mr Smythe that Miss van Knut was not at all a nice girl, and that she really ought to have been blackballed. Mr Smythe in reply asked what he could do. He had already done everything that he could to protect Society from being invaded by a horde of Americans, and he had failed. Besides which, the Van Knuts had been elected in America, and in America they were probably a kind of criterion of suitability. When he himself had been in America, he had found that conduct like Miss van Knut's was not only accepted, but even encouraged.

"I shall certainly never allow such a person in my house," said the Duchess of Man.

And the determination would have been more than reciprocated if the knowledge of each other's conduct had also been equally reciprocal. For Miss van Knut was extremely unworldly, and was quite unprepared to admit (even if she had known it) that an exalted position has not only its duties but its privileges as well, and that one of the most valued of these is an understanding that its friends will be suitably blind and deaf to, and ignorant of, certain events on certain occasions. Mr Smythe understood perfectly when to hide anything awkward with the sheltering cloak of charity, and when to exhibit it, magnified large through a telescope, to all the curious crowds that were gathered around. He knew exactly what Society would and would not stand from whom. But Society's standard was not Miss van Knut's. Her views of both conduct and opinion were formed quite independently of it. They not only did not vary in accord with discovery, but they were sufficiently unsuitable not even to vary with the person concerned; and therefore it is no wonder if Society looked a little askance at a young lady whose views defied its control, and did not courteously vibrate in response to its convenience.

At the present moment Miss van Knut was not troubling her head about the frowns of Society (if at any moment such frowns could ever have alarmed her); for she was scolding Darlington for his gaucheness in placing them both in a false position. And he was protesting that he had done it entirely at her instigation. After a little dispute, they finally settled that for the future they would be such good friends as to keep Mrs Denbigh in constant despair, and at the same time would be discreetly vague about any declared engagement.

"For if we were definitely engaged, we should have definitely to break it off after Claudia was all right—we should have to assign reasons and pretexts for having quarrelled, and all that kind of thing; and you know what a bore that would be," said Miss van Knut. And Darlington acquiesced—as indeed he always did; for when he remarked that he did not see the necessity for the conclusion, he was told if he ever spoke like that again, he would spoil the whole plot by forfeiting once for all the friendship of Miss van Knut.

Tottie, fluttering about through the groups, was busy collecting and depositing small drops of scandal. He was now heard exclaiming that he wanted a chaperon to take him to the refreshment-room, as he didn't understand Italian, and was afraid to face the waiters alone. The pantomimic actions with which he accompanied these words showed that they were intended for humour, and some people put on a smile in consequence.

"That sweet child is crying out for his nurse and his feeding-bottle," said Miss van Knut to Darlington.

Mawnan, who was standing by Claud, remarked that the youth made him sick, and added that he was positively a little Clodius.

To which Claud replied that he must not forget that Clodius had some brains, and that if any one here was like Clodius, he thought it was Flashington.

Claud then looked round; and seeing Claudia sitting alone, he walked towards her, and began to make that bodiless, soulless conversation which people seem doomed to construct together when there is a feeling of restraint between them, and they happen to meet in public as merely casual acquaintances.

He had talked on for some time, he himself hardly knew about what, when he heard a few sentences near him which made him start and listen.

One speaker said, " Is he furious ? " And the other one answered, " Yes, furious. The Cabinet have wired for explanations, and he is going back to England to-night." " But what did the paper say ? " asked the first. " Oh, the paper said that he had determined to give Home Rule to India, and that if the Cabinet did not approve, he would force it on them by means of agitation. Then it went on in the usual strain. Mr Cade explained that until India was finally given up, England would never really cease to be an aristocratic country. But with India once again free, and England absolved from the crime of holding down in bondage more than 250 millions of our fellow-men in worse than the chains of slavery — and so on, and so on—we should be able, once for all, to give up our so-called imperial policy (merely a policy for providing the imbecile younger sons of the upper classes with sinecures), reduce the navy, almost abolish the army, and turn our attention to those crying reforms at home ·which are so often neglected in order to interfere with our neighbours abroad. Cade is not only furious, but he says that he knows who has betrayed him."

Claud felt his heart almost stop. He turned to Claudia. "Have you heard what that man has been saying?" he asked, in a low voice.

"Yes; very much the same as you told me the other night."

"Then you did not repeat it, did you? I am sure that you did not," whispered Claud, in a voice so distressed it was almost a soundless cry.

"No, not a word," answered Claudia, simply. "You told me, you know, it was private."

Claud felt the clouds roll away, and his beating heart warming him once again, as he said, "Then he must have been betrayed by some one else. The paper seems to have given a very exaggerated account of what passed; for he is quite clever enough not to commit himself in that violent way, at first." Claud looked round the room, and found the 'Morning Gazette.' There, under the startling heading of—

MR CADE AND M. COURIER:

A HOME-RULE SCHEME FOR INDIA;

FULL DETAILS—

he was astonished to see that not only everything which he had heard was put down, but that there was at least a column and a half devoted to the interview. The report was exaggerated, and in many parts very incorrect; and yet Claud felt that it could not have been invented. One of the three people present during the interview must have repeated what passed there. Claud had told no one but Claudia, and she had respected his confidence. Cade would not betray himself; and therefore Claud decided that M. Courier must be the culprit. "Well, it is nothing to me," he said to himself. "He and Cade must settle their business between them;" and he dismissed it henceforth from his thoughts.

CHAPTER X.

MISS RATTLETUBS had not been idle since she came
to Pompeii. She knew that all this " effete Society,"
as she called it, was soon to be doomed to destruction—indeed she candidly told it so. Her triumph-
ant prophecies of its approaching dissolution almost
raised her to the rank of a female Jonah. Meanwhile she found it very pleasant to participate in
everything (under protest and with due denuncia-
tion) that was going on around. She was a great
political as well as a great social reformer. Her
friends said that she was a thoroughly dependable
" platform woman "—which meant that when any one
was getting up anything, to protest against something which they happened to dislike, she might
be relied on to take a chair on the platform and a
prominent part in the proceedings. She was pre-

pared to assist the Radicals in suppressing all liberty, and at the same time to protest against the State being allowed to enforce vaccination. She was anxious to convert every one to teetotalism, so that they might shut up all the public-houses at all times. She wished to see women with seats in Parliament as well as with a vote, in order that that body might be both more efficient and more expeditious than it is at present. She followed Mr Cade about, and tried to engage him in conversation; but he, for his part, generally tried to be engaged elsewhere. So she had to fall back on Mr Giles. "We women want to help in the fray," she used to say to him; "you might at least let us get into the Caucus."

Mr Giles thought that their most useful work would be influencing the people by agitation outside.

Miss Rattletubs agreed, and then proposed the brilliant idea that they should establish a Daisy League, to cut out that nasty ridiculous Primrose rubbish. She had, as we have before seen, a great belief in badges and ribbons, and other outward and tangible signs of inward regeneration. She was distressed that the whole delightful paraphernalia —the habitations, the titles, the badges, and the flowers—should be devoted to upholding such a vague and antiquated thing as the Constitution.

"If the Constitution can be supported by a primrose, it can surely be destroyed by a daisy," she cried; while she began vigorously to organise the league—or rather to try and organise it, for Pompeii proved obdurate; thus giving another sign of the degenerate and reactionary tendency of its patrons.

Even Mr Leo seemed to throw cold water on her plan when she unrolled it to him. He told her that he considered politics too serious and delicate a science to be intrusted to a league. And when she assured him that the Conservatives had gained a great many votes by theirs, he was disinterested enough to reply that even in that case there was no necessity to follow their example.

"The Constitution, as we have it at the present time, is the natural development and the logical sequence of the 'Constitutions of Clarendon.' We propose to abolish once for all the remnants of the feudal system (the remains of which still clog

our every action), and in fact to neutralise the
Norman Conquest.   Now do you think that a
Daisy League could accomplish this?" he asked,
in an airy voice.

"Of course that is just what a thoroughly practical hard-working league like this could and would
do," put in Miss Rattletubs, with brisk determination.   "We could throw ourselves into the cause,
and make it our very first business, as you
say, to agitate against, and to finally abolish, the
Norman Conquest."

But Mr Leo sadly shook his head.

Miss Rattletubs, however, found a warm sup-
porter in an unlooked-for quarter.   The brilliant
Flashington—who made it his business to be nice
to every one, including the most unpromising—had
taken Miss Rattletubs "up," as the phrase goes.
This effort was to him a more onerous one than
might have been expected; for it included the
acceptance of her "sanitary soap"—soap guaran-
teed on the label to be as "cleansing as a Turkish
bath."   He had even tried (once) her "non-alco-
holic, syrupy, temperance stimulants," and had
received, as a concession to male weakness, one of

her " anti-tobacco cigars (warranted to be entirely
free from the leaf of that poisonous plant)."

He swallowed these gifts (metaphorically) in
order to get the organisation of the Daisy
League under his control. He was just con-
verted to Liberalism (not having been won over,
we are sorry to say, by its obvious righteousness
and inherent truth, but by its present success and
the prospect of its future unconditional triumph).
He was determined always to be on the winning
side, no matter what that side might be; and it is
possible that in the future—even the near future,
if we progress at the present rate—the elegant
Flashington will be seen crowned with a scarlet
cap and leading a riotous mob on the West End.
At the present moment, however, anything of the
sort is premature; and therefore Flashington—who
loved above all things to be of importance—contented himself with hurrying about as though the
fate of the empire (which he was doing his little
—his very little—to injure) depended on his
exertions.

He was anxious to begin a " political career,"
and he foresaw that the Daisy League would be

the very thing to give him notoriety; for we know that nowadays notoriety is not only the first step towards success, but has come to supersede all other attributes, and is the one, and only one, quality absolutely essential to gain that end.

Flashington had seized an early opportunity for consulting with Giles as to his future conduct.

He had taken him for a long walk; and when they had found a shady nook beneath some trees, and Giles was provided with one of Flashington's own cigars, he opened the subject by asking Giles what was the best thing to do in order to get a " seat."

" I used to be a Conservative at Eton and Oxford; but I see it won't do any longer," he added, frankly. " The landed interest and that sort of thing are played out; and I mean to succeed."

" Capital—capital," answered Giles, giving him a friendly slap on the back. " I think we can manage to do something for you, if you go in for being extreme."

" Yes; I'll be as extreme as you like."

" It is better to begin as extreme as you can. You must be docile to your Caucus; but try, if anything, to go a little beyond them. That is the first rule for success. The second is, that you must be a thorough party man. Always vote with your leaders on all occasions, no matter what you've said, or what they propose — that is, of course, unless the Caucus tells you not to. Above all things, try and manufacture a ' mandate'; for if you can manufacture a ' mandate' you will be irresistible, and no Government will venture to refuse you anything that you may want. And there's another thing: I wouldn't, if I were you, be too conscientious—too scrupulous,—you understand me. For instance, if you've happened to state in a speech, for party purposes, that the Tories are in league with Irish traitors and murderers, and you have denounced them for betraying their country ; and then, if we happened to find it convenient a short time afterwards really to do what we had accused them of doing,—of course you would vote with your party, and say that events had changed, if it was necessary to say anything at all, which it wouldn't be, because the Caucus would quite understand that under the circumstances no questions had better be asked."

" Oh, of course !" said Flashington, cheerfully
(and we may do him the justice to believe that he
was already such a thorough " party man " that
what some old-fashioned people might consider the
dishonourableness of such conduct never for a moment struck him) ; " I know the great thing nowadays is to be practical. If one is too consistent,
one simply becomes *doctrinaire*, like the dear old
' Spectator.' "

" I used to take in the ' Spectator ' ; but I never
found that it did me much good, and now it's gone
and made a fool of itself too. However, to return
to our subject. If you're very extreme and very
active, you've no idea how fast you'll get on. All
the moderate men are passed over now ; and they'll
push you on, partly through fear and partly through
love, till you may find yourself in the Cabinet."
Mr Giles warmed with the congenial nature of
his theme. " Look at me ! I'm to have the next safe
seat. Well, I'm certain to be in the next Liberal
Government (they daren't keep me out if they
wanted to)—probably in the Cabinet; and though
I have risen from the ranks, I labour under the
disadvantage of not being a working man," added

Mr Giles, thoughtfully. "Well, you'll simply have to be all the more extreme, in order to cancel the disadvantage of your birth and training."

"Why shouldn't I go in for being a sort of Alcibiades?" Flashington asked. But Giles did not catch the allusion, so he continued—

"Learning and all that sort of thing pays sometimes. Look at Buckle, for instance. He's been popped straight into the Cabinet, not because he knows anything about public affairs, but simply because of his literary abilities." Giles was quite right. Buckle was a man who had passed most of his life immersed in study. He expressed, in an extremely brilliant style, his ideas on the philosophy of last century and the politics of this. His chief knowledge of life and affairs had been gathered out of the best books of the past, and then given forth in a few good books of the present. This (fictitious) Minister had been called "an up-stairs politician" by a sneering Tory—a trite enough joke, but perhaps as good as could be expected, when we remember that it is a commonplace of the other party that they possess a monopoly of wit and humour. He had probably already the drafts of two or three amended constitutions for England written out in pencil, and stowed away in his bureau. He gave the very finest literary finish to a Cabinet much in need of finish, and he displayed a dispensing policy, for which there was also a vacancy, by declaring that he should use his discretion as to when he should permit the law to be enforced and when allow it to be broken. "Lastly," said Giles, summing up, "always remember who are really 'the governing classes.' See what will tempt them, and promise them that. At the same time, keep the upper and middle classes amused with phrases; for if they once took fright and combined against the governing classes, where should we be?"

They went on to discuss the line which it would be best for Flashington immediately to pursue. He was to join the National Liberal Club at once,—Giles told him that Brooks's was much worse than useless,—and then the Committee would "run" him if they thought he seemed a likely man. He went back radiant at the prospect of being of so much use to his party and to himself; and the very next morning he started for England, in order to put his plans into execution.

The same afternoon Claudia, strolling along the beach, had fallen in with the children of the Princess Chioggia. They ran up to her, and implored her to tell them fairy stories, with all the demonstrative affection and unconscious grace of small Italians.

"You will tell us some more pretty stories, will you not?" the boys cried, themselves looking like little princes in a fairy story, with their long hair, their lovely faces, and their high-bred yet perfectly childlike bearing.

"And it must be quite true," added the tiny Princess Marie,—a child so exquisitely beautiful that she seemed to be of no distinctive type or nationality, but simply a little vision of almost angelic perfection, astray from some far-off world of poet's dream and painter's fancy.

Claudia smilingly assented. She seated herself on an old piece of timber, washed ashore from some winter wreck. She took Marie on her knee, and the boys clustered round; while she began to tell them the saddest and most poetical of all fairy stories—Andersen's "Little Mermaid."

They listened breathlessly when they heard how

the gentle little one rose up from her coral home
in the depths of the sea, to breathe the fresh air
and see the fair world above; how she loved the
beautiful prince, and saved him, his dear head
unconsciously resting all night on her bosom.
They thrilled at the dread and gruesome visit to
the awful sorceress, through that weird jungle of
horrid ravenous sea-plants that stretched out their
hungry arms, thirsting to suck her blood; and at
the burning potion that turned the poor little sea
maiden into a wistful, speechless, suffering woman.
And when the end came—when she sat on deck,
on through the long night hours, now hopeless,
still soulless, unloved, broken-hearted, and then
silently sank into the dark waters, to fade into
drifting foam—their eyes filled with tears. And
not till they learnt that the little heart of the
maiden had earned a soul at last, were they comforted.

The boys crept close to Claudia, and leant their
heads against her, with the pretty caressing ways
of Italian affection. "Tell us another—another
story," said the little Marie.

So Claudia told them the story of a little

princess who lived, once upon a time, in a vast
granite castle, far off in a distant country, where
endless woods sank away to unknown mountains.
A malignant, uninvited fairy arrived at her chris-
tening; and after the fairy had asked to kiss the
child, and was refused, she slowly said:—

"The first kiss that she gives will seal her fate for aye,
For either they must wed, or one of them must die;"

and then departed.

The king and queen dissembled their grief and
forebodings. They decreed that all kisses should
be henceforth punished with death, and the little
princess was brought up without knowing even a
parent's embrace. But she could not be wholly
reared as a virtual child-prisoner. So sometimes,
on the long summer days, they allowed her to
wander away into the woods, where everything
seemed to slumber through all the hot slow afternoon, lulled by the heat into silence.

One day when she was resting, for the warmth
had made her feel a little languid, she saw a poor
farmer's boy trying to carry a load too heavy for
his strength.

She called him to her, and asked him if he could not find some one to help him to carry his burden.

And when he had told her that he was an orphan, and bound to a cruel farmer, who treated him badly, she felt her heart fill with pity—for before this she had always believed that every one in the world was happy, or at least had an evening meal, and a soft white bed to sleep in—and she offered him, with a sudden shyness of shame, a little money (it was all that she had), to get himself something, if he could, that would comfort him, and perhaps remind him of her sometimes.

He looked up with his eyes swimming over with thanks, and told her that never before had he known any kindness—not even a kiss.

And when she asked him to tell her what that might be, he blushed, and answered shyly that when people love one another they kiss.

"Then you must kiss me," said the little princess. He looked at her with his hungry eyes filled with loving adoration, but he did not move —only the blush on his cheeks still deepened.

"You do not love me," cried the little princess.

A light leapt to his eyes, and swept downwards over his burning face, as he seized her hand and kissed it. Then the little princess leant forward quite simply, and gently kissed him on the forehead.

At that moment she felt herself snatched from behind. She was seized by a frightened attendant, and found she was being half led, half carried back to the castle. Her natural questions were answered by awful assertions — from which she gathered that if the kiss she had given were ever revealed, she would certainly die.

And so she concealed the remembrance, even as though it were some stolen treasure, far away in the lofts of memory, and guarded it there with silence, through the years that skim by so swiftly when winged with youth.

The years passed by; but the princess slowly faded, and her face was veiled with a delicate pallor. She lay, uncomplaining, all day on her little couch, like an ailing flower, shrinking by slow degrees, and life almost seeming to shiver away in her mute and drooping helplessness.

One night when the castle was hushed and
the hour was auspicious, the malignant fairy rose
up once more to affright the waking king and
queen with these muttered words:—

> " The princess has been kissed ; and as I said,
> She dies, or he dies, or the two must wed."

The king and queen, in terror and despair,
questioned and requestioned their daughter, until
at last she yielded up her secret, and they learnt
the dreadful truth.

They went forth, not trusting others with the
errand, and found the boy at work among the
hay — for it was early summer — mowing, and
singing to himself an old-world tale of love, as
the cool grass sank down before his scythe.

And standing there in the flowery meadow,
bright with the noonday warmth, they told him
that he must give up his life, or the little princess would die.

The poor boy looked on them awestruck, as he
might have looked upon avenging gods charged
with a Nemesis irrevocable and inevitable as the
tomb.

The memory of that golden day long ago had
always been to him like the love for some dear
companion, born in pondering day-dreams; and
now that he learnt that his life must be sacrificed to that one single kiss (for he was too
simple and faithful hearted to doubt or question
the king's assertion), he felt he could lay it down
as gladly as if it were given for friend or brother.
He only asked that some one might care for his
humble dog, giving it food every day and a shelter
at night.   And when they had promised, he added
a whispered request that before he died they would
let him see the little princess once more.

The following day, as the sun was setting, they
led him beneath the oriel window in whose shadow she lay so quietly, gazing with dreamy eyes
towards the rosy fires of the West.

The poor boy, with his dog at his heels, walked
very slowly, and gazed upwards with a wistful
adoration, as he would have looked had some
white-faced angel come down to him from the
bright skies above.

He felt, for perhaps the first time in his life, all the
sweetness of living—of simply being; and clinging

to life as he had never clung before, he was filled
with a sudden yearning that she would give him
but one swift look before he passed on—for ever.

She turned round; she saw the boy, and gave
him a smile of recognition. Lit up by the sunset,
to him it seemed divine in its radiance; and he
passed on to death, reconciled by the sweet thought
that she knew him, although she might never know
that her life was saved by his.

In a dank and tangled corner of the forest, he
found the cruel blood-red berries of a poisonous
plant. He carried them to the place where, on that
fair summer's afternoon, they once had met. There,
after he had eaten them, he stretched himself upon
the damp moss; only the slightest shiver, now and
again, proclaimed that he was entering into the
shadowy pathways of his final sleep. And when
the thin blue mist of evening floated up around
him, his loving dog still licked his face with dumb
reiteration.

As soon as the princess saw the boy pass by, she
felt a sudden rush of glad surprise, of happy recollection, and told her parents that he must come
and see her. She added that if he were by, if she

might sometimes talk with him, she thought she should get stronger soon. The king and queen, to quiet her, murmured, "Perhaps to-morrow." And when the morrow came, they still replied, "To-morrow."

The princess gradually grew stronger, and her parents knew that the spell was working and the curse was departing. One day, when she had wandered beyond her wont, she came across a little graveyard, quiet and overgrown — almost pathetically green with long desertion: only one grave was new, and on it lay a dog, weak but still faithful to his loving watch. She hastened forward over the rank impeding grasses to where the kind old dog was lying quite exhausted.

And then, suddenly recognising in him the one companion of his little master, she threw herself down upon the powdery earth beside him and covered his head with her kisses,—a stray tear or two, it may be, mingling in their fall.

She returned to the castle, the poor dog humbly following her, perhaps knowing instinctively that she was his only friend. But from that day she slowly faded; and at last, on one calm morning very early, she too entered into the dim land from which no mortal ever passes hence.

"And thus we see," said Claudia, in conclusion, "that if we shirk our duty and neglect our opportunities for doing kindnesses, in the hope of gaining some advantage, we still are punished for our selfishness."

"You tell us such sad stories," said the eldest boy. His eyes had filled with tears, but now were bright with returning expectation.

"Tell us something about giants and dwarfs," suggested the little maiden.

But Claudia got up, and answered that perhaps another day she would tell them funny stories. Now they had had enough, and she suggested they should walk with her back along the beach.

They had not gone far before they spied an artist painting. Claudia warned them not to go too near, as he was busy; and then, after they, not heeding her words, had run up to him, she saw that it was Redburn.

He looked up as though he had been caught in the midst of some of the occult tricks of his profession, and said, a little apologetically—

"I have only just begun—a little study, you see, of sea and shore."

"But we can't see any picture," cried the children, in all the frank outspokenness of childhood.

He looked up at them.

"Ah, I see you want some people and boats in the foreground," he said.

Claudia asked him quickly if he did not paint in the most advanced French style. And he answered that he supposed he was *dans le mouvement*, as the French say.

"Some of the modern French painters say they see no black in nature, and some cannot see any shadow; can they?" asked Claudia. "Perhaps soon," she added, "they will not be able to see any form either."

"Well, you know, I can't see outlines in nature; at least, I can't see any when I nearly close my eyes," said Redburn, cheerfully. "It's very convenient when one's drawing is weak; and one is able to give up the whole of one's attention to *tone*, to the *values*. Though, as Miss van Knut said the other day, 'She could conceive that, even in spite of that, my pictures might not have very much value after all.' But then, you know," he added, with a smile, "she laughs at Botticelli; so what can I expect?" For Redburn was a very rare example of a painter who does not take his own work too seriously, and who is quite prepared to joke a little at the expense of his own painting. When Claudia asked him if he had done much since he had been at Pompeii, he replied that he had only done a few little studies for Dowdeswells —"One must keep one's pot a-boiling, you know " —and that he had to start in a day or two, as they wanted him for polo at Hurlingham.

He turned back to his study—a grey-green sea against a grey-blue sky, with a grey-white foreground of sandy shore, upon which a few grey and ragged thistles, subdued to a right tone and a faultless *value*, stood out discreetly.

"Come," said Claudia to the children, "we must not hinder Mr Redburn any longer;" and the little party retraced their steps along the shore, with the sunset glow behind them, and the welcoming lights of Pompeii now beginning to appear as points of fire across the intervening stretch of sandy beach, to hasten their returning footsteps.

CHAPTER XI.

For several days after his interview with Mrs Denbigh, Claud had been unable to speak to his uncle about his future prospects, because that gentleman had been absent from Pompeii, having gone to Genoa for a little change of air.

One morning he discovered that Lord St Kevan had returned, by receiving a little note from him, which contained a request that he would be kind enough to visit him as soon as possible.

"Holloa!" said Claud to himself—"he seems as anxious to see me as I am to see him;" and he took up his hat and made his way quickly to his uncle's rooms.

He found him standing in what his irreverent nephews used to call "his senatorial attitude"— his feet slightly apart, his back well to the wall, and his hands stowed comfortably away beneath his coat-tails. "Young men nowadays don't know what to do with their hands," Lord St Kevan was wont to remark, "so they put them into their trouser-pockets. If trousers go out of fashion— or I should rather say, if trouser-pockets go out of fashion—where will their hands be then?"

This was the way he sometimes gave expression to his opinions, for it must not for a moment be supposed that he indulged in any language of the kind on this particular occasion. Claud thought that his uncle looked at him coldly, almost sternly, as he came in, and he began to wonder what his offence could possibly be.

"I am very glad you sent for me," he said, "because I have been wanting to speak to you, for several days."

"In that case, your affair shall have the precedence, as mine perhaps is both newer and less pleasant." Lord St Kevan's manner was perfectly courteous; but Claud seemed to detect a certain underground current of irritation, which he knew boded ill for his enterprise, and which from the outset had made him feel nervous. The old feel-

ing that he was going to make a fool of himself,
took possession of him. He always considered
that the sooner the plunge into anything disagreeable is made, the sooner it will be over; so he said
quite simply—

"I am in love."

"In love!" echoed Lord St Kevan, with only
the very slightest emphasis of exclamation in his
voice.

"Yes, with Miss Denbigh. I think you know
her a little. Her mother, to whom I have spoken,
said that—well, that she must know more about
my prospects before she could allow it to go any
further." Claud began to feel very uncomfortable, he hardly knew why, as he continued, "And
so I told her that I would speak to you about
them."

"Then she considers that your prospect of success at the Bar is problematical, and wants to
know if there is any securer basis for matrimony;
is that so?"

"I suppose so."

"You yourself," continued Lord St Kevan, in
his measured tones, with the seemingly inevitable

sequence of sentences following each other with quiet certainty—"you yourself, perhaps, also share her views ? "

" I am in love," repeated Claud — that at the moment was all he could think of saying; and then he added, "and of course I want to marry— to marry as soon as possible."

He knew that the remark was inconsequent; but he could not remind his uncle that he had always been treated and regarded by him, not indeed as his legal heir, because he was a second son, but as the heir to a large part of his private fortune. Yet his uncle seemed to be trying to drive him to this declaration, perhaps only to deny the assertion when made.

" You have been brought up with certain expectations, I know; but I also had reserved certain expectations for myself as well. For instance, I had always hoped that you would some day represent the family—the family interest and principles—in Parliament. I had hoped we might perhaps soon have been able to obtain for you some minor post in the Government; I had even ventured to hope that some day you might have formed an alliance

with one of our own families;" and the way Lord St
Kevan said "our own families" was an epitome,
as it were, of all the aristocratic traditions of his
race. "But you will find," he continued, "as I
have done, that in this life we are doomed to
disappointment."

He walked two or three times up and down the
room; then he stopped in front of Claud, and said
in a changed voice, "I will write to Mrs Denbigh;
but my answer to you will perhaps depend on your
answer to me."

He took out a letter from his pocket, and his
voice became drier and drier—so dry that it might
have been extended before some internal fire—as
he said, "I have received this letter this morning
from Mr Cade; perhaps you can explain its con-
tents to me;" and he handed it to Claud. It ran
as follows:

"DEAR LORD ST KEVAN,—When I was at Pompeii
the other day, I had a private interview with M.
Courier, at which your nephew Mr Brownlow was
the only person present besides ourselves. In the
course of conversation I expressed to M. Courier

my hope that at some future date we might see our
way to giving India a certain amount of autonomy.
Four days after this, a long and exaggerated account
of the interview appeared in the 'Morning Gazette,'
although it had been perfectly understood that the
conversation was of a strictly private character. The
Cabinet were extremely annoyed ; and though the
'Daily Letterpress' inserted a paragraph, at my sug-
gestion, wholly denying the truth of what had been
stated, I was forced to return to England in order to
furnish them with explanations. I have long known
that malignant lies and unscrupulous dishonour
have been the determining factors of the Tory policy ; and I should not therefore have been surprised
at your nephew's betraying me, or, indeed, have
troubled you with this letter, had I not felt that it
was a duty to inform you, an old and valued member
of our party, that your nephew, in deserting the
principles of his family, has also abandoned their
practices.—I am, yours truly,   WILLIAM CADE."

"How dare he write such an impudent letter
—such an impudent letter—as that ! As though
I should condescend to publish his confidential

treason in the newspapers!" Claud was trembling
with fury and excitement. He had sprung up long
before this.

He was now beginning to tear the hateful letter
into fragments.

"I wish to keep that letter," said Lord St Kevan
quietly. "I know that in asking you if it were true,
I was merely complying with a form. For I am
sure that you could have told nobody what had
passed." Then he added, "Of course I am right in
my supposition; you have told nobody?"

"Nobody—nobody except a young lady," said
Claud.

"*Except* a young lady!" The tone again had
altered. The emphasis was ominous.

"And she has told no one. I will stake my life
on that."

"In telling that young lady such a secret, you
did a dishonourable act. I do not know if your
new Tory principles are such as Mr Cade has
stated—are part and parcel of that party—but this
I do know, that whether your young lady did or did
not respect your communication, I shall never be
able to reply to Cade that you have repeated his

conversation to *no one.*" Lord St Kevan's voice was
becoming almost fragile—hard and thin, with the
stress of suppressed emotion—and seemingly brittle,
as it came forth cooling from the furnace of his indignation. " I shall have to apologise to *that man*
for the ungentlemanly, the dishonourable conduct of
my own nephew." And then the clear thin voice
trembled and suddenly broke, as he added, " It is
the most humiliating moment of my life."

Claud felt both distressed and indignant ; furious
with Cade, and even a little angry with his uncle,
for he knew that the report in the newspaper had
not appeared, either directly or indirectly, through
his words to Claudia. To Lord St Kevan, with his
old traditions of statesmanship, and his exquisitely
delicate sense of what was honourable in public life
(probably a survival which had defied obliteration
by the recent actions of his party), any private information from a member of a Government was the
most sacred of communications. His professional
sense of what was fitting was outraged ; and he was
overwhelmed with shame at having a nephew who
could repeat to a lady a piece of confidential information, even though both he and she were innocent

of the newspaper article which had followed in this instance. He had known important secrets confided to ladies once or twice in his career before, and he had always found them followed by profound catastrophes.

Claud was the first to break the momentary silence. " I think you are not fair to me," he said. " I did not understand that the conversation was particularly confidential. I have only repeated it to one person—a lady—who assures me that she has not said a word about it to any one. This article has probably got into the paper through something Cade himself has said; and, instead of apologising for your nephew, I hope you will reply that you cannot permit him to be insulted."

Lord St Kevan could not help admiring Claud's spirit. He himself was as furious as Claud—perhaps, if possible, more furious—at the tone of Cade's letter. But this was the very reason why he was maddened by the knowledge that he could not give it an indignant and absolute denial.

" For the first time in my life I shall have to humiliate myself—to humiliate myself to that creature, to that impudent brazen cad;" and Lord St

Kevan began to lose control over himself—an occurrence so rare with this stately and courteous nobleman, that Claud might well be a little scared.

"Don't condescend to answer his letter at all," said Claud.

"I shall write, and I shall apologise. I shall apologise for my nephew's conduct in having foolishly repeated some portion of the conversation to a lady," said Lord St Kevan, with a certain air of almost dogged deliberation; for his strict sense of duty and of rectitude would not for a moment permit him to pass over these details in silence. "But I shall add," he went on, "that I have reason to believe that the report of the conversation went no further; that the paper obtained its details from other sources; and that, although my nephew may have deserted the principles of his family, Mr Cade 'is the last person who could convince me that he had also deserted its practices, even though he had joined a party which Mr Cade honours with so much abuse." He got up and again placed himself in the senatorial attitude before he went on—"As for your future, I shall of course continue the allowance I have always made you; what may happen at my death remains to be seen—it will probably depend on your future conduct. But you must not look to me for encouragement, either pecuniary or otherwise. Speaking of your marriage, I think you are too young, and I think that a few more years' work, before you settle down, would be invaluable —invaluable to you. And therefore, as far as your future prospects are concerned, we may conclude that they mainly depend on yourself and your future exertions." He sat down; he had evidently finished. Claud murmured something which he believed sounded like some form of thanks, and in a moment found himself once more in the blinding sunshine and the busy street.

He felt crushed; he felt that he had been unfairly, unkindly treated. And yet he hardly knew why. His uncle had only proposed to tell the literal truth to Mr Cade, before defending his nephew from insults and insinuations. Lord St Kevan believed in his innocence, as far as the newspaper was concerned. It was only his own momentary indiscretion that was so cruelly magnified by his uncle's morbid sense of the honour of confidence. "Then again," he said to himself, "how can I complain of my uncle's intentions about my future career ? I have not chosen to walk in the path he had planned, and how can I expect him to smooth my way ? " And Claud even added— for he was extremely sensible, and was almost capable of that rarest of tasks, the more or less impartial judgment of one's own actions and interests— that Lord St Kevan's views were on the whole very sensible. Why should he not work ? why should his whole future depend on the will, it might be on the caprice, of another ? But all this time a knell was ringing in his ears and tolling in his heart —a knell foretelling with a dread and iron certainty the death of all his hopes, the silent funeral of all his future happiness. "He has crushed me," cried poor Claud; "and now I know my love is impossible." And the knell seemed to take up the word "impossible," and jangle in with it "irrevocable" and "implacable," with a dreadful and continuous reiteration.

Lady Marlowe had planned a picnic for the afternoon of the day on which these events took place. Claud had been asked; but now he wondered with a dull indecision whether he should go or not. As

the time which had been fixed for starting approached, he had not troubled to make up his
mind; and he would probably have remained behind, seated on a marble bench in the Forum, with
an unread book before him, and his eyes unconscious of its proximity, had not the volatile Miss
van Knut and her father happened to pass him on
their way to the gate.

"Well, you do look glum," said that young lady.
"You seem to have been badly left this time, any-
how. Aren't you coming around to this picnic?"

Claud shook his head.

"Oh, come on; it will smarten you up to skip
round a bit."

"But you will have Darlington to skip round
you," answered Claud, it must be admitted a little
morosely.

"Hear him!" cried the young lady to her father;
"hear him talk about the son of a great peer of the
realm" (she rolled out the words with a tinge of
comical gusto, as one might if one spoke about
a mighty mandarin of the Celestial Empire) "as
though he were a puppy dog!"

"My, Eliza, the way you talk! You are really

losing your high tone in Europe," remarked her father.

But Eliza, not in the least abashed, remarked, "Here comes his lordship," and made Darlington a curtsey, such as ladies give to a royal prince when he shakes hands with them, and which she pretended to think it was "the thing" to bestow on Darlington when he came forward to greet her.

" Really !" said Darlington.

" You needn't look so mad, Lord Darlington. I learnt it from the greatest authority on high life here, I assure you. Always curtsey so when honoured by being shaken hands with by a prince of the blood or a royal duke." And she imitated Mr Smythe's manner and mode of speaking (with just the slightest hint of his provincial accent) as she gave a second little illustrative curtsey.

" Mr Brownlow is moping here by himself. You must get him to come to the picnic, Lord Darlington."

" Oh, come along," said Darlington, taking Claud by the arm and preparing to pull him off the seat.

So Claud, seeing that resistance, if not useless,

would at any rate be more troublesome than acquiescence, got up from the seat and sauntered on
beside Mr van Knut. Miss van Knut and Darlington seemingly considered that their duty was
accomplished, and therefore indulged in the pleasure of walking on ahead together.

At the gate, they fell in with the rest of the
party. They all started for the hills, with most of
the ladies mounted on donkeys, and the men either
walking beside them, or else plodding on in friendly
couples.

The afternoon was lovely; the air was warm;
the grey olives in the midst of the sunshine filled
the view with their delicate silver glitter, and as
the languid breeze passed over them they seemed
to throw off a soft green shimmer of pearly light.

The party passed vineyards and dark-leaved
orange-groves, delicate scanty grass—already a
little browned by the sunshine—amid which the
wild flowers glowed and sheltered. And ever behind and below them, as they scrambled up the
little mountain-pathway, was the sapphire expanse
of whispering waters, that now so serenely reflected
the measureless blue of the sky above.

Lady Marlowe rode on with the Duchess of
Man. Their conversation was fragmentary, and
was mostly compressed into more or less ex-
clamatory remarks on the beauty of the view,
the heat of the weather, and the stumbles of their
animals.

When the sophisticated reader has been informed
that Mr Smythe was among the company, it is
doubtless needless to tell him by whose side that
gentleman was progressing.

He was now engaged in ingratiating himself with
the Duchess, and in transforming the slightest of
acquaintanceships into a reliable friendship. Although he was the "jack of all trades" of Society,
and was accepted, nay, even encouraged by it, in
that capacity, it still possessed individual members
who looked upon him coldly, and considered him a
stranger, or (to use his own word) an "outsider."
The Duchess was one of these. She "did not know
Mr Smythe." She assured all her friends that she
did not intend to know Mr Smythe; and in spite
of reciprocating his remarks with a certain (small)
share of her own conversation, she would probably
declare the very same thing to-morrow. For one

of the many advantages of being in Society is, that you can have pleasant and even intimate talks with a person, without being subsequently obliged to know him or recognise him in any way, if you fancy that you may be thought rather smarter for not doing so.

Then came Mr van Kaut, chattering cheerfully about "The Central of New Jersey Consolidated bonds" to a perspiring gentleman, who mopped his face and absorbed financial information with equal gusto.

Claud walked on by himself, and tried to turn over his future career in his mind. The sunshine and all the brightness around helped to focus it into a dark contracted vista of sunless chambers, mouldy books, and stifling courts, in which he played the supernumerary part of a briefless spectator: a helpless struggle through long years, eternally dragged on amid the fogs of gloomy London. This prospect, as he formed and pictured it in his mind, was not of the most cheerful character. But at the present moment, the prospect of meeting Mrs Denbigh was even more dispiriting. He hardly knew whether the absence of

Claudia from the party was a relief or an additional cause for depression. And so he walked on by himself mostly, with his head filled with gloomy forebodings, and only now and again exchanging a few words with any one near.

The party found their lunch prepared for them amid the shadows of some spreading trees — the servants had preceded them — and everything looked additionally tempting after the long scramble in the fresh air. The gentlemen divided their attention between indulging in the meal and assisting the servants to wait on the ladies. Jack de Barry was in "great form." He settled himself on one side of Miss van Knut (we can guess who was on the other), and was most assiduous in providing for all her wants.

"We want to make you feel at home," he said.

"Well, you are really both so attentive, that I can almost fancy you are Americans," she replied.

"Think of that now," said Jack. He was a little shocked; but not being very quick at repartee, he simply inquired if all the young men of New York did not have to send bouquets to all their young lady friends.

"Every toney young man who respects himself does so. At least he sends them to all the belles that are going to the same dance as he is. And then they take us the loveliest drives. In Europe the horses don't even seem to know how to trot."

"When I come over to the States, you'll take me out drives behind a trotter, won't you?" said Darlington.

"Unless you are very good, you won't have the privilege of being treated in the American way." Then she looked round. "Pa!" she cried out to her father, "here's Lord Darlington asking me to drive him about America behind a trotting horse."

Mr van Knut was quite undisturbed; he merely looked up—"You bet," he said, and went on with his lunch.

Some of the ladies also looked up; their eyes met—startled flashes of shocked intelligence passed from one to another. Mr van Knut did not see them, and would not have cared if he had. But his daughter intercepted and translated them with instinctive accuracy. She swept the whole company with one defiantly inclusive glance, as she said—

"In Europe, papa, you're suspected if you are too confiding or too polite. I see I must teach you how to behave in the European manner. You should have said, 'My dear, I will drive Lord Darlington round, if he is good enough to honour our cottage with his presence. You perhaps will be allowed to speak to him at the dinner-table, when your aunt is there as a chaperon.'"

Mr van Knut was somewhat puzzled by the tone of his daughter's words. However, he contented himself by saying, "Well, my dear, if Lord Darlington is good enough to come and stay with us, I guess he would rather that you drove him around and amused him than that I did," which did not exactly mend matters.

His daughter turned to Darlington with a shrug of her shoulders, "You see how impossible it is to educate one's parent up to European propriety. I cannot get him to understand that I have to be always guarded from you by a dragon in the form of a chaperon."

"I am sure I should like America awfully," said Darlington, simply.

Lady Marlowe was very much amused at this

bold defiance of all the conventionalities of Europe. "She really is a most extraordinary girl," she whispered to the Duchess. "And yet, you know, one cannot call her vulgar."

"But I can, and I do call her vulgar—indecently vulgar," said the Duchess, impressively.

"She is really the simplest and best-hearted girl in the world," said Lady Marlowe.

"Too simple to hide her scandalous fastness," said the Duchess.

"She is too simple to hide anything," said Lady Marlowe. "But I assure you she is anything but fast; indeed you would be surprised how prudish she is about many things."

"She is *not at all* a nice girl," said the Duchess, in her most oracular tones, which, combined with a superincumbent stratum of manner, simply finished any argument with a kind of blank cliff of assured conclusiveness.

Tottie, who in his small way sufficiently valued the friendship of duchesses, sat on her other side. He now saw an opportunity of engaging her in conversation, and began to fire off a succession of foolish phrases (which he managed to get accepted as jokes

by some people). He jerked them out with his
head a little on one side and his arms crossed, each
hand nursing the other's elbow—an attitude much
affected by certain young men in London. They
ran on somewhat like this: "The goose which this
paté is made from was fed entirely on tallow candles, I'm certain—not too much goose, but just
enough tallow." ("Isn't he fun!" whispered Lady
Marlowe to the Duchess.) "I'm goin' to a fancy
ball at Nice next week. I shall go as a ballet-
girl,—I think it will be so *chic*. I daresay I shall
get lots of flowers and things given to me. I shall
want a wig; I might borrow Lady Beechwood's.
I could whisk it—woof!—off her head when she
wasn't looking" (and he imitated the action while
he spoke). "Then, when I came back, I could set
up a scarecrow with it and one of Mrs Leo's gowns.
They say she makes 'em herself. Just a piece of
stuff sewn up like a sack; though I s'pose it
doesn't matter, when all the figure she has is
wrong side before. The other day she said to me,
'What do you think of Turner?' I said, 'Good
gracious! what's that?' She said, 'Oh, he's a man
—an English painter.' So I said, 'Oh, I thought it

was French for a dress-improver.' She said 'I really don't know what you mean.'· So I said, 'Ask your grandmother.'—No, thank you; I daren't eat any more, or I shall bust one of my own stay-laces," said Tottie, refusing another helping of *pâté*, with a giggle as he spoke.

By this time the meal was over. Every one got up; the men had lit their cigars or cigarettes, and people began to stroll about. Some started on a further climb, to see the view from a height a little above the spot where they had been lunching; others went to pick wild flowers; others again preferred to stay and rest amid the cool shadows that slanted across the grass from the sheltering trees above.

M. Courier was one of the latter. His expansive bosom (or, to be strictly truthful, perhaps the word should be changed to figure) was embraced and confined by a black frock-coat. He was smoking a cigarette with all the national relish. He looked the picture of solid and satisfied comfort as he stood there with his face to the view and his back to the climbers. He seemed suffused with a warm geniality, all in accord with his general air of genial

warmth. No one could have guessed that he was
an advanced Radical, dissatisfied with the state of
society (not only Society with a big S, but the great
society all around us that only claims a small one),
and that even republican France looked on him,
more or less, as a dangerous demagogue.

M. Courier, then, was warming himself in the
sunshine, at the moment at peace with all men—
for even the man who persuades himself most that
he is a sacrificed martyr to civilisation, sometimes
enjoys himself in this most tyrant-ridden of worlds
—when he found himself touched on the shoulder
by Claud. He received him effusively, for his
French environment filtered his manner from
everything short of extreme politeness. He expressed himself charmed to renew an acquaintance commenced so felicitously; and when Claud
suggested that they should confirm its renewal
with a gentle stroll, he again was charmed at the
notion, and took Claud's arm with a certain impressive urbanity.

He plunged at once into the midst of his favourite
topics. "Your statesmen," he said, "are wanting
in ideas."

"Mr Buckle has ideas," said Claud.

"And therefore you mistrust him," said M. Courier.

"Yes; we think him a dangerous man," replied Claud. "The English people do not like being governed by a man who has ideas. They prefer to be governed by a man who has race-horses."

"Strange people, you English," said M. Courier. "And yet you flourish—or perhaps I should say, have done so, for I mistrust your future."

"There is danger ahead; for 'the ideas,' I am afraid, are gaining on 'the race-horses.'"

"Mr Cade assures me that, with the advent of democracy, an entirely new social system is being evolved."

"It is just about Mr Cade that I have been wanting to speak to you," said Claud, breaking somewhat roughly into the train of thought. "You remember the conversation the other day about Home Rule for India. It seems that Cade regarded it as more or less confidential; so that when an account of it appeared in a London paper he was furious, and accused me, in the strongest, and I must say the most unscrupulous terms, of having betrayed him." Claud began to feel that perhaps there was a certain want of judiciousness in the way he was stating his case, considering that his great hope was that M. Courier would be able to acknowledge the indiscretion as his own. So he changed his tack. "My uncle, Lord St Kevan," he said, "was extremely annoyed about it; and as I am anxious to put myself right with him, I thought I might venture to ask you if you had any idea how—how the article came to be written?"

"My young friend," said M. Courier, expansively, "you will find that everything, *everything* appears in the papers nowadays. I know nothing about the article."

"But did you tell no one?" persisted Claud.

"I may have done so. I cannot remember."

"Perhaps some lady?" suggested Claud, remembering that in his own case it was assumed that to tell a lady such a piece of news was regarded as much the same thing as trumpeting it one's self to the general public.

"I think I did tell Mrs Denbigh—at the ball. Ah yes; I recollect," said M. Courier, in his easy comfortable way. Not in the least realising how

much he was adding to Claud's happiness, far less
conceiving that he was helping to remove a stain
from his honour, he went on with his cheerful talk.
They chatted about Paris. M. Courier described
the latest opera bouffe, and the new comedy at the
Français. But to Claud, though he listened and
answered occasionally, the whole stream of their
talk seemed to flow on and over him like a stream
of music. A weight had been lifted from off him;
his whole nature had wildly rebounded, and had
soared up to find in the surrounding sunshine the
most perfect expression of its unspeakable relief.
He had obtained at the same moment a shield to
disarm attack, and a weapon for use if one should
be necessary. He almost skipped along by the
side of the portly Frenchman. He found himself
singing a little French song, and when his companion said, " Please continue; that is one of the
best of all Judic's *chansonnettes*," he permitted himself to sing it aloud, and even to mimic that clever
lady with an imitation so lifelike and ludicrous
that M. Courier burst out laughing.

"Ah! you have spirits," he said.

And Claud's spirits indeed seemed to flash and

dance with the dancing sunbeams. He felt them rising and bubbling over, in tune with the boiling kettle that purred a recall to the warm and refreshing tea it was promising. And they finally winged his feet into running races with some of the others over the flowery grass on their homeward scramble.

PRINTED BY WILLIAM BLACKWOOD AND SONS.

www.ingramcontent.com/pod-product-compliance
Lightning Source LLC
Chambersburg PA
CBHW020055030726
47498CB00006B/1797